Also by Jan Springer

Intimate Lover
Intimate Kisses
Intimate Stranger

Kidnap Fantasies
Jade's Fantasy
Zero To Sexy
Christmas Lovers

Pleasure Bound
A Hero's Welcome
A Hero Escapes
A Hero Betrayed
A Hero's Kiss
A Hero Wanted
Captive Heroes

Pleasure Bound Boxed Set
Pleasure Bound : COMPLETE SERIES SciFi Erotic Romance Boxed Set

Tentacles Shifter Erotic Romance
Taken by Him

The Desperadoes

The Pleasure Girl

The Key Club
A Merry Menage Christmas
Sophie's Menage
Jewel's Menage
Jaxie's Menage

The Outlaw Lovers
Jude Outlaw
The Claiming
Colter's Revenge
Tyler's Woman
Resistance
The Outlaw Lovers
Alpha Outlaws Boxed Set

Vampira
Sweet Heat
Dark Heat
Wet Heat
Crimson Heat

Standalone
A Touch of Menage Boxed Set
Shades of Menage Boxed Set

Naughty Girl Desires Boxed Set

Nice Girl Naughty

Sinderella Sexy

The Biker and The Bride

The Fire Within

Bared to Him

Pleasure Bound : A Futuristic Adult Romance Boxed Set

Merry Menage Kisses Boxed Set

Inner Girl Rising

Stripped Naked

Risqué Girl Delights Boxed Set

A Holiday Menage

Ménage À Trois

A Hitman for Hannah

Billionaire Boyfriend

Edible Delights

Vampira

Toygasm

The Dark Side

Watch for more at www.janspringer.com.

The Pleasure Girl

The Desperadoes Series
Book One

*S*olar *flares have disintegrated most of Earth's human population, frying electrical grids and thrusting everyone into a cold, harsh land where only the strong survive.*

After the catastrophe, Teyla Sutton becomes a pleasure girl, entertaining men on her secluded Canadian farm. When she accommodates dangerous desperado, Logan Leigh and his two friends, Spencer and Cassidy, pleasure becomes addictive beneath their tender touches and their hard, muscular bodies. What she never expects is to fall in love...

Logan shouldn't allow the pleasure girl into his heart, but he knows it's too late because she's already there. He and his friends have put their lives into danger by hiding out at her farm. They're on the run. They need to leave, yet Logan wants her so much. Dare he risk his heart and their lives to be with her?

Soon Logan, Cassidy and Spencer are whisking Teyla away on an exquisite journey into her hottest desires and forbidden fantasies. But when she learns the trio are members of a notorious outlaw gang, can she allow them to stay in her life, or will she send them away forever?

Copyright

License Notes

This eBook is licensed for your personal use only.

Author Note

This is a work of fiction.
Characters, places, settings, and events presented in this book are purely from the author's imagination and bear no resemblance to any actual person, living or dead or to any actual events, places, and/or settings.

Chapter One

L ogan Leigh sat on his black stallion and peered down at the early
morning frost covered valley below. A lone spiral of gray smoke
drifted from one of the several rock chimneys of an old white clapboard
two-story farmhouse and to his surprise, an unusual warmth sifted
through him at the thought that this place felt like he was coming
home. Weird that he would think that way of this valley nestled in the
Rocky Mountain foothills of Alberta, Canada, a place he'd never seen
before, but that's what he felt.

The warmth of the sight urged him to hurry up and ride down
there, but he knew the dangers for a man on the run. He needed to keep
an eye on the place and make sure there were no surprises when he rode
in. Aside from laundry fluttering in the cold breeze on the line, there
appeared to be no sign of movement. Experience, however, cautioned
him that looks could be deceiving.

Members of the gang he rode with had told him a pleasure girl lived
alone down there and despite the insistent hardening of his cock at
finally having some female companionship, he knew he'd have to force
himself to sit up here awhile longer until he was sure they wouldn't be
interrupted by a posse.

Then he'd ride in.

It was getting dark fast and she needed to get cleaned up at the
water pump and grab her laundry off the line before it got too creepy
out here, Teyla Sutton thought as she struggled to close the damaged
greenhouse door. The darned hinges had been ripped off several weeks
ago during a violent windstorm and the plate glass door was so heavy

she could barely move it, but she knew getting the door into the proper position would keep the heat from escaping the building and so she struggled with it until it gave a good, closed fit.

Wiping a bead of perspiration off her forehead, she wrapped her thick wool cardigan tighter around her and headed into the chilly wind toward the water pump in the middle of her farmyard. She'd been working inside her greenhouse for most of the day, planting a new crop of carrots and Boston lettuce, weeding, and watering the rest of the plants and enjoying the moist warmth compliments of a southern exposure of the building as well as the solar heating.

But out here in the gloomy evening, it was a different story. Since the Catastrophe over four years ago, the weather had turned cold. Sure, the sun continued to shine during the day, but it just wasn't warm enough to grow most crops or any flowers anymore.

Since the weather had turned bad, she'd had to make do without pretty much everything. Food at the store in town was priced out of her reach so she'd turned to growing her own food in the greenhouse. She fished or hunted her meat and got her water supply from the well. For her there was nothing but healthy organic living these days and she was lean, thin, and healthy because of it.

But boy she could kill for a large double double coffee and a plate full of apple fritter doughnuts about now. As if her tummy knew exactly what she was thinking, it growled in protest, the spooky sound sending another volley of shivers up her spine, making her think of a growling grizzly bear ready to pounce on her from behind the nearby pine trees, encouraging her to pick up her pace.

She didn't like being outside when it got dark. Every shadow became a potential murderer and every sound became a pack of wild dogs that could be lying in wait ready to rip her throat out and dine on her. Despite the spooky shivers racing up her spine at her vivid overworking imagination, Teyla forced herself to smile at her silliness.

She'd been lucky since the Catastrophe. She didn't get unexpected visitors because most humans had been disintegrated, thanks to the deadly solar flares. Many of the survivors tended to live in what was left of the cities and they didn't really bother with her way out here in the foothills. She had, however, heard rumors of cannibal gangs roaming around killing and eating people because meat was just simply too expensive for the average person. Those cannibals stayed mainly in the populated areas where the food, so to speak, was more accessible.

At the pump, she quickly pushed the squeaky cast-iron handle up and down until the chilly water splashed out. Grabbing the bar of homemade lye soap, she kept beneath a tin cup; she hurriedly washed her hands and face, shivering in the cold breeze. Thrusting a bucket beneath, she filled it with water.

Once she got inside, she'd get the fire roaring in the woodstove and wash herself more intimately with warm water. Yes, she had solar water heating in her farmhouse but she preferred to use it only when necessary because if her solar parts broke down, they were too expensive to replace or even get for that matter. So, she tended to play pioneer with her water, lugging buckets and heating her water on her kitchen woodstove.

She was about to lift the full bucket when a jolt of alarm ripped through her, stopping her cold. At the sound of a horse neighing, her head snapped up and shock and fear snapped through her as she saw a big man wearing a black leather jacket and tight blue jeans quietly leading a black horse into her yard not more than forty feet away.

Oh darn! Why hadn't she seen him coming?

She forced herself to remain as calm as possible. Forced herself not to make any fast moves in case he went for the rifle in his scabbard. But her fingers sure did ache to reach for the gun sitting heavy and loaded in her cardigan pocket.

"Can I help you?" she called out, wishing her heart weren't pounding so violently against her chest.

"Mrs. Teyla Sutton?" he asked.

He spoke quietly as if trying not to spook her, but damned if she wasn't ready to either run for the farmhouse or start shooting at him.

"That's right," she answered, cursing herself for the shakiness in her voice. Okay, so he knew her name. That was a good sign, wasn't it?

"Your neighbor, Dr. Elizabeth Brandywine sent me. I'd like to purchase your services for a couple of days."

Her services. Despite the frigid air lashing her face, her cheeks went warm. Why would Liz send a stranger to her? Teyla preferred to service only men she knew. Men from town. She had no idea who this guy was.

"She said you might also accommodate my two friends."

Her breath backed up in her lungs. Two friends? And him?

"I don't accommodate strangers. I'm sorry."

"She's already inspected me if that's what has you worried. My friends will be here tomorrow."

Teyla shook her head, fear starting to really grab hold now. What if he got violent for refusing him? Why in God's name would Liz send her a stranger?

"She gave me this note to give to you. It gives me a clean bill of health," he said.

She tensed as he took a couple steps forward and handed her a sealed envelope and when he did, she didn't miss how large his hands looked or how long his fingers were. They were clean, his nails clipped. It was a good sign and showed the man took care of himself.

Opening the envelope, she relaxed as Dr. Liz's delicate scent whispered off the page and her familiar handwriting explained that she'd done a physical on him, and that he appeared clean and he came recommended by a trusted friend.

"A letter of introduction, I would assume?" He grinned down at her and Teyla's tummy flip-flopped quite nicely at the man's succulent smile.

"She says she knows a friend of yours. I don't normally service men I don't know, so this doesn't make me eager to take you on as a client. Mr.?"

"Logan Leigh," he offered. "I'm from the States. Crossed the border a few days ago."

His smile widened, and it reached his dark brown eyes, making them sparkle with amusement and heat. That latter thought had her thinking sex with this guy might be worth breaking her usual rules.

"Before you give me your final decision. I want to say I'll give you five times your rate for doing my two friends and myself."

Her eyes widened at his generosity. With that amount she could buy those pickling seeds, mason jars and pickling salt she'd been dying to get and down her beets and cucumbers when they were ready. Not to mention pay off several months of her mortgage.

But have sex with a stranger? And two others?

She swallowed at the nervousness shifting through her.

But all your clients were strangers in the beginning, an inner voice whispered at the back of her mind.

Confidence edged away her fear. Liz had sent along a letter of reference and stated he was in good health. Teyla needed the money and having sex with men was her job. So why was she hesitating? Because it was too unexpected and he looked too damned sexy, that's why, that inner voice whispered again.

Sighing in resignation, she nodded to her water pump.

"You can wash up here. Give me about fifteen minutes, then come in. The bedroom is at the back of the house, just off the kitchen. Please leave your weapons in the kitchen and I need to have half the money up front."

"My horse?"

"You can put him in the barn to protect him from the coyotes. There's some feed in some bags left over from my horse. It should still be good."

She didn't explain her only horse was dead and buried just last week. None of his business that she didn't have any sort of transportation anymore. She grabbed her bucket and started toward the house, hoping he wouldn't pull out a gun and shoot her in the arm or worse. His next words stopped her cold.

"We haven't discussed the terms yet," he said softly.

She tensed, placed the bucket on the ground and turned around again readying to grab her pistol from her pocket if necessary.

"I do anal, oral and vaginal. Condoms are necessary. No kissing on the mouth," she said trying hard to keep the huskiness out of her voice. God, just talking sex with this guy was kind of exciting.

"Bondage. I want to do some bondage on you, plus you'll have to accept three men doing you at the same time or there's no deal."

Three men at the same time! She'd never done *that* before.

Before she could mount a protest, he held up a hand.

"We want access to all of you, whenever we want for tonight, tomorrow and tomorrow night. You'll get half your money up front. The other half at the end of the second night. You'll wear no bra while we are here. You'll dress the way I want you to dress. The first night is just us then tomorrow and tomorrow night will be the four of us. The next morning we'll be gone. Is that acceptable to you?"

Teyla couldn't believe how warm her cheeks had gotten at what he'd said or how nervous she'd become too.

She'd never agree to bondage. They could tie her up and slit her throat or torture her and she wouldn't be able to defend herself.

"No bondage. No pain," she said firmly

"No pain, and only your wrists bound. Your legs will be free."

"Yeah, like that'll help me if I need to fight you off."

"You'll be too busy fighting the pleasure. Mrs. Sutton."

She blinked at the sultry way his deep gravelly voice whispered through her.

His smile dropped into a serious frown.

"Mrs. Sutton, if I wanted to harm you, I would have done it early this morning when I first saw you hanging up your laundry."

"Maybe you need an audience," she replied, tartly, feeling spooked at the thought he'd been lurking around here all day watching her and she hadn't even noticed.

"I enjoy watching a woman get taken by another man and I enjoy an audience when I'm taking a woman."

He certainly got to the point, didn't he?

If Liz sent him to her then Teyla would have to trust he wouldn't hurt her. She just wished Liz could have come herself with the guy and made the introduction. She shook away those thoughts. She was acting like a child. This would simply be a business transaction. No emotions. Just like all her other clients.

"We'll see," she said and she noticed the heat flare again in his brown eyes. She'd expected an argument but he was pleased with her answer.

"I want you to wear what's inside this package."

He held out a linen wrapped item which she reluctantly accepted.

"I want you wearing it and sitting on your bed waiting for me."

She nodded. Without another word he turned away, grabbed the reins of his horse, and walked toward the barn.

You'll be too busy fighting the pleasure. Oh my gosh, had he really said that? My oh my he was a confident one in his abilities, wasn't he? None of the men she'd serviced had made her feel anything. She just went through the motions and pretended she enjoyed the sex. It would be the same with this guy, she thought as on the weirdest trembling legs, she headed for her farmhouse, walking a little bit too quickly for her comfort.

After bedding his horse in the barn, Logan grabbed one of his saddlebags, emptied out the money, counted half the amount he promised and stuffed it into an empty feed sack. He eyed the interior of the barn for a good hiding place for the rest of the money and decided on putting it into the hayloft on the second floor. After the money was secure, he grabbed one of his saddlebags and the feed sack with her money in it then headed out to the water pump where to his surprise he found a folded towel, face cloth and a new bar of soap. The woman must have brought out the supplies while he'd been in the barn.

He gazed at the farmhouse and was pleasantly amused to catch sight of the woman studying him from one of the lower floor windows. He grinned and waved, enjoying how quickly she disappeared after being caught watching him.

She was the cutest pleasure girl he'd come across. Her hair had been brushed messily to the sides as if she'd been wiping her hair back off her forehead through the day. She looked to be just about as tall as him and as old as his thirty-three years. Her eyes were deep brown and her lips were full and very kissable looking. And he swore she'd blushed in the twilight while discussing the terms of their arrangement.

What was up with that? A pleasure girl blushing? Dr. Liz had assured him this woman had been in the business for at least a couple of years and would most likely accommodate him and his friends.

Well, whatever the blushing was about, she'd agreed to some of his terms. Now all he needed to do was wash up. As he grabbed the handle of the pump, he couldn't stop but gaze around at his surroundings. Shadows were dropping throughout the yard as the golden sun dipped past the snow-capped mountains to the west.

While he'd been keeping an eye on the place during the day, he'd noticed the barn roof needed reshingling, saw that some of the fences were down and the rusty windmill squeaked with every gust of wind.

Now upon closer inspection, he noticed she was struggling just to survive out here. The farmhouse looked in relatively decent shape but it could use a hand of white paint and a couple of blue shutters needed to be fixed before they fell off, but the farm equipment as well as the truck were covered in dust. He understood why too. The solar flares had fried most vehicles' systems. Those vehicles that had been fixable ran into the problem of gas, which was hard to come by.

The Catastrophe had fried the entire world's electrical grids, the solar flares short circuiting pretty much everything from nuclear plants to the Internet. He'd heard of the odd nuclear plant melting down Stateside and realized he'd probably been exposed to radiation fall out and maybe his healthy days were numbered, but it was all out of his control, so he just took life one day at a time.

Understandably it was taking a long-time in training survivors as replacement workers for the various factories that made parts needed to get the coal plants, nuclear plants, and other electricity producers up and running again. The lack of electricity had thrown cities, towns, and villages into the dark ages. Looting was rampant. Prices for food and water were skyrocketing.

It seemed everybody that had the ability to make a buck had no problem exploiting the people who needed help. He didn't like what had happened to humankind. Didn't like what he'd become either. Wasn't proud of the kind of work he had to do in order to help the less fortunate. Unfortunately, his work was illegal and now he was a wanted man.

He inhaled sharply as frigid water dashed onto his hand.

Wow! But it was like ice! How had she been able to wash her hands and face earlier? Hell, if she could do it, so could he. Determination made him pump harder. Grabbing a nearby basin, he filled it with water and dumped the washcloth in.

Removing his jacket, sweater, and T-shirt, he shivered in the frigid air, inhaling and cursing as he slapped the wet washcloth and bar of soap against his skin and began washing himself. It was the middle of June and it felt like a mild winter day.

Chilly weather year-round. It was another drawback of the Catastrophe. The weather had changed worldwide. They were calling it the Little Ice Age, due to the lack of sunspots, which, after the explosion of solar flares had burned out those sunspots that gave the Earth its added heat, thus lowered temperatures on Earth were a direct result. So much for the greenhouse effect.

Logan frowned and reached for the towel. He didn't want to think about the Catastrophe and what happened right after. That dark time had changed him and made him bitter. He did, however, want to think about that sexy piece of lady in that farmhouse. Right now, she was the one bright spot for him over the next couple of days. He would lose himself inside her.

At the thought of all the sweet things he would do to her tonight, his cock hardened. He was going to enjoy taking her. Enjoy it a lot.

Teyla was trembling as she slowly moved to the bedroom window again. He'd seen her earlier watching him and getting caught had sent the oddest tingles of excitement through her. There was something about him that made her breathless, but in a good way. Something that made her want to watch him. Maybe because now that she was a little less freaked out by his sudden appearance, she realized he was the handsomest guy she'd seen in a long time. Or perhaps because that smile of his when he'd caught her spying on him made her feel so giddy. Made her believe he wouldn't hurt her.

She peeked out and watched him as he washed his upper torso in the twilight. Muscles rippled across his shoulders and arms as he soaped his hairy chest. He was a big man, she thought as she licked her suddenly dry lips. A very tall man with feathery, shoulder-length light brown hair.

And he wanted *her* services.

She hadn't slept with a stranger since first starting out as a pleasure girl more than two years ago. And even those men had been familiar to her. She knew them from church or church gatherings or at the hardware or grocery store. Some had been friends of her husband. Some just acquaintances. Those had been the lucky ones who hadn't disintegrated, just like her. Sometimes though, she wondered who exactly had been lucky. The ones who'd gone poof in a second to ash, or the ones left behind to mourn and struggle.

She blew out a tense breath as she watched the newcomer's hand draw toward the clasp on his jeans. His head snapped up and before she could move away from the window, his gaze captured hers again. Once again, the wicked tingles zipped through her at getting caught and that cute smile of his as he looked at her made her cheeks grow hot.

Chastising herself for being a peeping Thomasina, she moved away from the window. She needed to hurry and get ready. Rushing back into the kitchen to the woodstove where she'd left some water to warm, she grabbed the pot and headed back into her bedroom. She'd wash up in a minute. First, she wanted to take another peek at Dr. Liz's note.

Liz said he was a friend of a trusted friend who vouched for him and he was looking for her services. Liz explained she'd given him the required physical exam and gave him a clean bill of health. Because Teyla had been so flustered at the stranger she hadn't read the rest of the note explaining to her that Dr. Liz would give his two friends physicals too when they showed up and would send along another letter. It was the last sentence that totally caught her attention. Liz asked her to let her know if size really did matter?

Goodness, couldn't Liz have been more specific than that? Size meaning, he was too small? Two big? Too long? What?

Dammit! As if her heart wasn't racing now at the thought of finding out. She glanced out the window again, and a very erratic butterfly feeling splashed through her lower belly upon discovering he was now totally naked. While washing his lower half he'd turned his back to her, revealing a very cute ass. She hoped he hadn't been offended at her gesture of leaving the soap and other items out for him, but he'd looked dusty and she figured he'd like to wash up before...

Oh lord, Teyla! Stop delaying.

She really needed to hurry and get herself ready. Ripping her gaze from him, she quickly lit some of her oil lamps on the shelves in her room, undressed and washed herself, and gave her wrists and neck a few delicate squirts of her precious perfume.

Then she opened the package he'd given her and gulped at the gorgeous white lace material. It looked beautiful; she thought as she lifted it up and gazed at it.

It was sexy. Smashing. He'd given her a sheer floor length negligee set. By the fresh smell and look of it, it was brand new.

Whispering the delicate material through her fingers, she moaned at the silky softness. She hadn't touched something this soft in years. She also noticed the side slit would reveal her left leg and hip. A thong panty accompanied the garment too. The panty had a large hole in the middle allowing him access to her...

Another shot of warmth into her cheeks made her swear softly beneath her breath. Oh boy. Could she go through with this? Could she let a complete stranger, have sex with her? Share her? She should be running in the other direction, not getting all these mixed emotions raging through her.

Want, need, a craving to be loved.

Slipping on the panty, she sighed at the velvety feel against her skin, then moaned as she put on the negligee. It melted against her curves like liquid milk. Admiring the garment's beauty in the mirror, Teyla smiled. It looked awesome.

The top clung to her breasts like a glove, illuminating them, making them look bigger and the waist was gathered making it narrower than it really was. The lower part shimmered like ribbons of silk over her hips and legs.

Having something new made her feel almost normal again.

She jumped as a noise at the side of the house snapped her back to reality. He was coming! The sound of stomping feet ascending the outside stairs and crossing the wraparound veranda planked floor had her biting her bottom lip with a sudden bout of anxiety. A quick knock and a creak of the screen door followed by the other door opening, had Teyla hurrying to sit on the bed. Normally, she climbed naked under the covers and waited for her clients that way, but this man was different. He'd given her something to wear, and he would like to see it on her.

Her anxiety mounted and she clasped her hands into her lap as she heard him enter her home. Her sanctuary.

Chapter Two

Indecision continued to snap through her. Should she go out and meet him? Check if he had the money? No, he would have the money. Dr. Liz said he came recommended. There shouldn't be a problem, so she would be the demure sexual object he wanted.

Something heavy hit her kitchen table, making her tense. His saddlebag? Her money?

She could hear him breathing in the next room. The sound loud and raspy, as if he were aroused at being in her home. She'd left the bedroom door open and she listened intently. There were a few moments of silence and then her heart picked up a magnificent speed as his boots thudded against the wood plank floor of the old kitchen floor.

She thought he was coming into the bedroom but then she relaxed again as she heard the creak of a couple of cupboard doors opening. She almost called out to him asking if he needed something, but then the tinkle of glass and something being poured drifted through the air.

Another couple of minutes of strained silence drifted by and Teyla could only sit and wonder what he was up to.

And wait.

Soon the rustle of clothing followed, and she inhaled deeply to steady the frantic pounding of her heart. Suddenly, he began walking toward the bedroom door. Toward her.

Oh dear. Here we go. She held her breath. Tensed.

He appeared in the doorway with a bottle and two glasses in his hand. He wore his jeans and a black T-shirt. He looked good. Broad shoulders. Narrow waist. Lean hips. Sex-on-a-stick stud.

His dark gaze latched onto her and fire screamed through her veins at his potent look. Desire flared in his eyes as he studied her. His intense look screamed sex and she could feel her body answering with a raw awareness she swore she'd not felt before.

"Shaving gear. Where do you keep it?" he asked.

"In the adjoining bathroom. Second drawer to your left." She sounded too breathless. Bedroom breathless.

He nodded, ripped his gaze from her and strolled into the bathroom. Her nervousness mounted as she listened to a drawer opening.

What was the matter with her? Usually she was so cool, calm and in control with her clients. But with this guy she was both nervous and giddy with anticipation at the same time.

"Do you have a special man in your life?" The question erupted from the bathroom rocking her world.

"Excuse me?" She called out, wondering exactly what he meant by that question.

"A boyfriend? Husband? Someone you're dating?"

"N...no,"

"Good. I prefer a woman who is available."

Teyla blinked in astonishment. Odd comment coming from a guy who wanted to share her with two other guys. Three guys and her? Oh lord she'd better not think about it.

"Do you do this often?" she blurted, instantly regretting asking the question, realizing it was none of her business. But it was the first thing that popped into her mind and when she was nervous, she did have the tendency of saying stupid things.

He appeared at the doorway, shaving utensils and a couple of facecloths laid out on a folded towel in his hand. That damned bottle and two glasses clutched in his other hand.

He was smiling at her. That hot sexy shadow making him look both dangerous and erotic at the same time. He wore that same crooked smile as when he'd caught her watching him at the window earlier. The smile made the sides of his eyes crinkle and she noticed tiny laugh lines at the corners of his mouth also. The knowledge that he appeared to be used to laughing made her feel so much better. Safer too.

"Why do you ask?" he asked. "Are you jealous already?"

Sense of humor. Definite asset.

"Maybe," she teased, feeling some of the tension ease out of her shoulders.

He strolled to her dresser with the mirror and placed the glasses and the bottle, which she noted as whiskey, and the utensils and towel down beside her pitcher.

"Before we begin, I want you to shave me," he said softly as he prepared the items, laying them out on the dresser.

When he finished, he looked at her and his intense gaze made her catch her breath. She didn't want him to lose that erotic looking five o'clock shadow. It made him look so sexy and dangerous. The look excited her. But he was paying her. If he wanted a shave, so be it.

She made a move to stand, but he ordered her to remain sitting as he whipped up the lather. When it was a frothy cream, he turned to her and to her surprise his hand fell to the stud on his jeans.

Nervousness fluttered through her again. Gosh, she thought she would have a few minutes more before they had sex. Or did he want her to shave him while they were having sex? Lordy, now that would be interesting.

"I... I thought you wanted a shave?"

Her eyes latched onto his fingers as he unzipped.

"I do."

She swallowed as he lowered his jeans. His package pressed boldly against his white briefs. Definitely big. Very big. Oh boy. Oh boy. Dr. Liz girl, what have you gotten me into?

"I want you to shave me down here," he said and stroked the outline of his big erection.

Her eyes widened at his words.

Down there? Oh-my-God.

"I'll pass you the items. I want you to just sit right where you are." His voice had gone deeper, hoarser. His eyes darker. They glistened with fire. His body scent, strong and dominant, whispered along her nerve endings making her very aware of her sexuality. Very aware of him.

"Pull down my underwear. So, we can get started."

Both their breaths shot through the silent air like rockets and her fingers trembled as she did as he asked. His flesh felt scorching hot to her touch as she slipped her fingers beneath the waistband of his briefs. Tugging, she inhaled sharply as his giant, purple-flushed cock sprang free. He was already rigid, exceptionally long and so damned thick that her pussy creamed at the intoxicating sight. As she pulled his briefs lower, his sack, swollen and huge, appeared.

Oh yeah, a big guy. Now she fully understood Liz's letter.

She slid the briefs lower over his thighs and knees and she let them drop to the floor where he stepped out of them, moving closer to her. She realized her cheeks had grown warm. *She* had grown warm.

Down there, he'd said. He wanted to be shaved around his cock and balls. She'd never done that to a man. Not one of her clients had ever asked. It had never occurred to her to do something like that. Should she voice her inexperience? No, she needed to appear professional. Professionals knew what they were doing, and they followed a client's instructions. Especially if she wanted him to come back, and with his generous size, she wanted him to come back.

She accepted the prepared brush from him. He inhaled as she slapped the lather along his hairy parts. Noticed his gut clench as she feathered her fingers around his cock, lifting the heavy shaft to lather the fine hairs beneath. She held onto his solid flesh longer than necessary, enjoying the way he throbbed against her palm.

Next, he handed her a throwaway razor. That item didn't belong to her, so he must have brought it. Throwaway razors were another thing that were a luxury for her, so she tended to re-use the ones she had until they were totally dull before tossing them away.

Taking a deep steadying breath, she set about doing the intimate chore. His pubic hair felt fluffy and fine, a total opposite of her late husband's, which had been wiry and coarse. Anxiety almost overwhelmed her as she began to shave him and she found herself scrambling for something to say. But what did one say while shaving a man in such an intimate area on his body?

"Have you done this before?" he asked, his voice sounding strangled, as if he were maybe afraid? Well, maybe he should have asked before she'd gotten started?

"It's a little late to be asking that question, isn't it?" She couldn't help but laugh.

"I hope not," he retorted, amusement lacing his voice. There was that humor again. She smiled and lifted her gaze from his magnificent size to peer up at his face. She shouldn't have looked up because his eyes were so dark with desire, she could barely stand the spear of need bursting inside her lower belly.

The tips of his luscious lips tilted upward again and his smile zeroed in on her like a heat seeking missile. Suddenly she just wanted to be swept away into his strong arms. To be held. To be taken by him.

Oh boy. He was a client, for God sakes! Becoming emotionally involved, even thinking emotional things was taboo! Men looked at her like an object. Nothing more. She shouldn't want to have Logan holding her and making love to her. This was just sex, remember that Teyla.

She continued with the shave, going slowly and carefully, and keeping her mouth shut. Thankfully, he said no more and when she finished, she wiped him with the wet face cloth he handed her. A couple of rinses later, he was as clean as a newborn.

"I assume you wish to supply the condoms?" he asked after he returned the shaving items to the nearby dresser. She nodded and pointed to the night table beside the bed.

"In there. Pick your size." He slid the drawer open and skimmed the several boxes with his fingertips. Obviously, he knew the drill with pleasure girls. Most preferred to supply the condoms. She was one of them.

Condoms were expensive, just like everything else these days, but well worth the expense to ensure her condoms were fresh and hadn't been tampered with or inadvertently damaged by men who tended to keep them folded in wallets or kept in areas where tiny holes were inadvertently poked into the protection. The last thing she needed was a sexually transmitted disease or a baby without a dad.

He lifted out a box of condoms, opened it, but didn't take any out.

"Before we begin, let's get a little more acquainted. You've touched me and seen some of me. Now it's my turn. Let your breasts free."

To her surprise, she creamed at his instruction. She liked the expectant look on his face and for some reason he didn't make her feel like she was dirty as she usually felt with her other clients. He didn't make her feel like an object. He just made her feel kind of sexy and shy.

Her fingers trembled as she reached for the small delicate buttons on the negligee. His Adam's apple bobbed as he watched.

She'd undressed in front of her clients many times. Had felt embarrassed as the men eyed her as though she were a piece of succulent piece of meat. It was the opposite with this guy.

She was ogling him. And she liked what she saw. Liked the sweet shivers of anticipation rolling through her as he watched her unbutton the top. His breath was the only sound she heard, aside, of course, from the pounding of her heart.

She swallowed, and opened the sides of her top, tugging the material further apart, allowing her breasts to spill free. He said nothing, but his facial features told the story. Appreciation glazed his eyes. His nostrils flared like a bull's and as she dropped her gaze from his face she was greeted to a most magnificent sight.

His cock which had already been sticking straight out was now rising proudly toward his abdomen. Such a glorious size.

She hadn't realized she'd been so mesmerized staring at his cock until he whispered in a hoarse voice, "Nice. Very nice."

A savage look of lust zipped across his face and she whimpered a deep guttural sound as he dropped to his knees in front of her. He maneuvered closer to her legs, his hands dropping like heat waves on her knees. He parted her knees and he moved in closer. Positioning his hands on top of hers on each side of the bed, he held them captive, his fingers intertwining with hers as his head dipped toward her right breast.

Sweet mercy, she couldn't believe this was happening so fast. He opened his mouth and she cried with surprise at how tightly he sucked her nipple between his firm lips. A waterfall of magic swept through her. That's the only way she could describe the cascade of shimmering sensations washing over her as he sucked on her nipple. This felt amazing. Incredible.

Heat and pressure kissed her flesh, and when he suddenly let go of her nipple with a loud pop, she cried out her disappointment and caught the pleasure twisting his face before he latched onto her other one.

"Oh God," she hissed.

More of those incredible sensations shimmered through her as his strong teeth held her tender nipple hostage and his tongue lashed her flesh with quick sharp darts that had her creaming harder.

Usually, she didn't like to touch the client. Usually, she let them do what he needed to do, so she could get rid of him quickly. She'd just lay back and let her mind wander to other places, but this man wouldn't let her mind wander and he wouldn't let her body wander either.

Damn him, he held her full attention as he sucked her nipple slowly, leisurely pulling her out of herself. She arched against him, losing control in the glorious sensations. She sucked in a shock breath as his hot hands let go of hers and slid his calloused palms under her breasts. He cupped her, held her so tenderly that the gesture wrenched a sob from her. No man had held her so affectionately. Not even her late husband.

The clients came and they went. They used, and they paid, but this man needed her in a different way than just sex. She didn't know how or why she knew that exactly but she sensed it somehow.

She didn't realize he'd pushed her down on the bed until she felt the mattress touch her back. Letting her nipple go, he kissed the tips of each of them. The beauty of his mouth suddenly became lost as he danced his lips with feather light caresses across her chest and up along her shoulder blades.

Then he came over her. He didn't touch her, didn't lay on her, just kept kissing her flesh, but she sensed he wanted more than kissing her body. They had just started and she already knew he wanted to break her rule. No kissing on the mouth.

"Logan," she warned as his mouth touched a flaming lash of heat alongside her chin.

"You said not on your mouth," he whispered.

He kissed his way to her right ear lobe. Sucking it into his hot mouth, she gasped as tidal waves of sensations hit. He bit her lobe, then laved her flesh with his wicked tongue.

Oh shoot, now she wished she didn't have that no kissing on the mouth rule. She parted her lips and inhaled at the incredible sensations zipping through her as he licked a fiery line down along her neck.

Then suddenly he cursed softly and without warning angled his head over her face and kissed her full on the mouth.

Bastard! She thought numbly as his lips melted over hers bringing her into a heady world of sensations. Vaguely she realized if she wanted to, she could break the kiss. She could push him away.

But she didn't want to.

She shuddered as he swept aside the bottom half of her negligee and his hard cock pushed into the opening of her panty and against her clit, giving the promise of pleasure, but then he moved his cock away again, leaving her frustrated.

"I like submission," he whispered, as he broke the kiss and her pussy clenched at his comment.

Wrapping his hands around her wrists, he brought her back up into a seated position.

"I want you on the floor on your knees," he said.

Her senses whirled at his command. He helped her to her feet and she swallowed and shivered. Trembled, not with repulsion as she always did with the others, but with this odd sense of curiosity. She became more aware of him now. Noticed the scent of the soap he'd washed with. The whiff of the prairies. Of him. Spicy, fierce, and needy.

The air grew heavy around her and she got into position on her knees in front of him. Reaching out, she slid her hands onto his hips feeling a bunch of muscles as his flesh met her palms. She slid her hands to his backside and cupped his hard ass.

He was breathing rapidly, and to her amazement, exhilaration lashed her at the thought of having his large cock in her mouth. Need thundered through her. A need to please. To be pleased.

She moved her head toward him. Toward his cock. His cock head was plum shaped and appeared flushed red. The skin felt so smooth as he pressed against her lips.

"Take me in as far as you can go," he ordered. "Nod when that happens."

She parted her lips and he sunk in, his hard flesh sliding over her tongue, his guttural groan saying he liked the feel of her mouth wrapped around his flesh. To her amazement, he stretched her lips like no other man had before. Stretched until her lips felt bruised and her body tense with awareness.

She nodded her head and he wrapped his hand around his shaft, preventing him from going in further. His other hand slid into her hair and he clenched the back of her head, holding her there. She tried to tighten her lips around his hot pulsing flesh, but he was just so unbelievably big and hard. He pulled himself out and her tongue dashed against the heavy veins beneath his cock as he left. He plunged into her mouth again and she hollowed out her cheeks giving him a nice big suck.

He groaned. Held her head tighter, obviously enjoying her sucking.

Surprise slashed her as she realized she loved his hot strong flesh thrusting out and back into her mouth. She slurped on his shaft, stroked him with her tongue. Looked up and watched the enjoyment flash across his face, saw his eyes close and his lips part as he panted.

His cock jerked violently in her mouth. He kept thrusting and she caressed his thick flesh with her mouth loving the wondrous throbbing deep inside her pussy.

"I'm coming" he warned.

His hands tightened against her head and he thrust into her mouth faster, more desperately. He groaned and his hips jerked against her as he thrust deeper.

She struggled to take more of him. He pounded into her. Again, and again until she was whimpering as she imagined how strong and powerful his thrusts would be when he took her vaginally. In one swift jerk, warm semen pulsed into her throat. It tasted thick and she swallowed quickly and sucked his cock. Milked him until he was moaning. Then he pulled free and Teyla warmed as she noticed his cock was still hard and he breathed in raspy gasps.

"Up on the bed," he panted. "On your back. Knees up and spread."

Her heart swept into wicked fast mode at his instruction. He grabbed her wrist and brought her to her feet. She made a move to get out of her negligee, but he shook his head.

"Not now," he whispered.

To her surprise, he leaned in for another kiss. Sensations rocked her as their lips melted together and she realized she'd forgotten to slap him again. He broke this kiss and nodded to the bed.

"In the position," he ordered.

She licked her lips, tasted his semen, and lay down on the bed near the middle. Lifting her knees, she saw her breasts jiggle as he climbed up at the foot of her bed. Between her legs, she watched him climb toward her.

He'd removed his shirt and his naked body was bronzed in places that really shouldn't be tan. It appeared he sunbathed in the nude. The thought vanished when he lowered his head and the vibrant need to be taken by him flared through her as his hot breath blasted like a furnace against the opening in her panty.

Heat and moisture swirled between her thighs. God, she knew she shouldn't be wanting this so badly, but she did. She shouldn't be opening her legs with such ease, without feeling the least bit hesitant or embarrassed, like she usually did.

Her belly clenched as his face nuzzled between her thighs.

She moaned as something hot and moist touched her clit. A finger? She wondered. No, his tongue.

He licked her clitoris. Up and down with firm, unrelenting pressure until waves of exquisite pleasure pulsed and she dug her hands tighter around the comforter as he continued lashing her tortured clit. Beneath his face, she writhed and gyrated and dug her heels into the mattress.

Hot sticky moisture seeped from her pussy and Teyla gasped, her eyes widened with wonder as he thrust two fingers into her soaked pussy. His fingers were exceedingly long and felt so good as he continued to work her ultra-sensitive nub with his tongue and thrust into her with his fingers like a cock. He sucked and she cried out as his teeth nipped her clit sharply, then his tongue smoothed the hurt, bringing lashes of pleasure through her core.

She groaned as he grabbed her by the hips and brought her pussy closer into his face. Every nerve ending inside her throbbed. She jerked, cried out as a third finger slid into her. The penetration stretched her in such a good way she bucked as shudders of arousal slammed into her.

She was about to come. Hard.

He gripped her so firmly she cried out in both fear and wonder as the magnificent orgasm began to take hold. But he let go of her pussy and disappointment and desperation made her reach out and grab him by the shoulders, trying to bring him closer again.

He shook his head. "Condoms, baby, condoms." he gasped, and she let him go, wanting him inside her. Needing him.

Her pussy was on fire, and she thought about bringing herself off. But the tearing of plastic and foil had her touching her nipples. They were nice and tender from his mouth and her breasts felt firm beneath her palms. She yelped as the mattress moved and he climbed back over the foot of the bed.

Grabbing her thighs, he pulled her down until her ass almost hung off the edge. She swallowed tightly as he moved between her thighs. He came up and over her, his thick cock reaching toward his belly.

His thighs widened hers as he came down. His hard gaze pinned her to the mattress. Strong muscles bunched in his arms as he angled his body over hers.

She struggled to make sense at how intoxicating his look made her feel. His face appeared so taut; his eyes so dark with intense need she instinctively knew he hadn't been with a woman in some time. At that thought hunger raged through her. An unfamiliar need she hadn't experienced before shot so deep into her she moaned at its intensity.

Then she trembled as his thick bulging cockhead nudged against her vaginal opening. He entered her swiftly and without mercy, her muscles stretching wildly as he impaled her. He filled her to perfection, his size reaching an area deep inside of her. An unexplored area that always wept with need when a man had sex with her.

With this guy there was no disappointment. Only awe as he withdrew and thrust into her again.

Once. Twice. Three times.

She unraveled, jerked violently as the orgasm exploded through her.

His mouth melted over hers catching her cries. His heated shaft slammed into her over and over. His pubic bone stroking her clit exactly right.

She rolled from one climax right into another one. He continued to thrust and kiss her. The only sounds were that of his flesh slapping against hers and their erotic moans. Oh, she did love the way they sounded as the sounds of their union mingled through the air.

She rode with him. Rode the waves and then finally she heard him whisper he was coming. His body went rigid and he shuddered, the condom filling with his warm semen. She felt him come up part and shift into his own world of bliss. Afterwards, in the drowsy after sex mode, her pussy spasms slowed and he withdrew.

Through heavy lidded eyes, she watched him as he carefully removed the condom and tied it off, then he tossed it into the waste basket she kept nearby for such purposes. The afterglow weakness of sex tugged at her and she felt fantastic. She wanted to curl up and go to sleep, but he climbed onto the bed, bringing her up beside him.

To her surprise, he spooned against her back side, and curled his arms around her, holding her against his hard body.

The thick knot of his cock pushed against the crack in her ass as he held her. For a long time, she hoped he would slip his cock into her pussy from behind. He didn't, and yes, she felt disappointed, as his breathing slowed. She thought he'd fallen asleep, he'd been quiet for so long, but then his deep voice cracked through the twilight's buttery glow of lamplight, his question shattering the comfortable silence.

"Where were you when *it* happened?"

She knew he was talking about the Catastrophe. Wondered why he would ask such a question at a time like this. Maybe he was trying to find out a connection they shared? Heck, everybody who survived shared the same connection. Losing their loved ones. Or maybe it just small talk on his part?

Whatever his reason, The Catastrophe, as everyone called it, was something she tried really hard not to think about. It was still very painful. Yet, Logan's question brought it all back in vivid detail, and suddenly she ached to tell him.

Needed to tell someone who seemed to care at least a little about her. Maybe because he was the first guy who actually thought about her pleasure instead of just his own. Maybe that's why she sensed he cared. Or maybe it was because he was her first client that she didn't have to fake an orgasm with?

"The day started just like any other," she began. "The sun was shining brightly..."

Excitement pummeled Teyla as she drove out of the town's mall parking lot with the truck cab full of two weeks' worth of groceries and the early pregnancy test kit sitting in the paper bag right beside her on the seat. Glancing at herself in the rear-view mirror she couldn't help but smile at her flushed pink cheeks or her windblown shoulder length wavy brown hair. Not one for wearing makeup she looked a mess, but at the moment, she didn't care because she just might be pregnant. For real.

When she'd stepped out of the farmhouse this morning, that same weird nausea kind of feeling was anchored in the pit of her stomach. She'd been feeling a bit sick intermittently over the past week. At first, she'd thought she had a touch of the flu, but then she'd had a light bulb moment. Morning sickness?

As she watched her husband of eleven years working in the lush purple lavender fields, she'd barely been able to contain the bubbling happiness of what she suspected. She dare not raise Max's hopes again only to find out it was a false alarm. It had happened three times over the past two years since they'd begun trying to get pregnant.

The look of devastation on his face depressed her for weeks and it made her feel like a failure as a wife because she knew he wanted a lot of kids and so did she. This time around though, she was playing it nice and cool, at least in front of him. That is, until she found out for sure whether the early pregnancy kit gave her a positive reading or not. If it did, she would go to the doctor and have it confirmed this time before she so much as uttered a peep.

Trying to keep her mind off her excitement she forced herself to gaze at her prairie surroundings. As always, the sparse dots of farmhouses, silver silos and fields of round hay bales baking in the sunshine soothed her rattled nerves.

Heart Creek was a bustling farm town of five thousand people nestled in the foothills of the Canadian Rocky Mountains. It had a main street with a grocery store, a bakery, a hardware store, two restaurants and one mall. It also boasted the only outside drive-in theatre for miles. This area was her home and despite having a three-year stint as a grocery cashier in the busy city of Calgary, Alberta, after finishing high school, she'd come back home to marry her high school sweetheart, Max Sutton.

She'd never regretted her decision but she sometimes wondered if Max did, especially when she caught him gazing longingly at their relative's endless stream of kids.

Since their lavender farm was around fifteen miles from town, it didn't take long for her to swing her truck off the paved highway onto the dusty road that bordered their five hundred acres.

They'd named their place Heart Pond Farm due to the huge man-made pond her husband had created about half a mile from their two story three-bedroom farmhouse. She could hardly wait to get home and hoped Max was still out in the fields so she could sneak into the house and take the test.

With her excitement rising, her fingers tightened on the steering wheel and she gazed over the sparkling purple fields on both sides of the dusty road. They'd planted lavender over the last five years, finding it an extremely profitable venture compared to the mustard, corn, and hay they'd grown before. The crop was ready to harvest and the sweet smell drifted into the open windows teasing her nostrils. She thought she saw a trail of dust in the east field and spotted a metallic glint. Slowing her truck, she braked and let the engine idle while she listened.

Birds chirped cheerfully, the wind whispered through the lavender plants and she smiled as she heard the grumbling purr of the tractor. Yep, he was definitely in the east field. Good, now she could sneak into the house and take that pregnancy test. With renewed urgency, she pressed the gas pedal.

Soon she spotted her white clapboard farmhouse huddled between a handful of huge pine trees and a moment later she'd pulled the truck into their parking lot. She was just about to shut off the engine when the bright flash of orange light sliced through the otherwise light blue noon sky almost blinding her. Intense heat rocked her and the truck stalled.

She could only sit there on the bench seat and stare out the windshield, stunned, as she swore, she saw the sky waver momentarily.

What the hell had that bright light been? Lightning? Why had the sky wavered like that?

She shook her head; her heart racing like it had never done before. She thought about twisting the key in her ignition but had this really bad urge to just get out of the truck. But if the truck had been hit by lightning, how did she get out?

Frig it! What did one do to get out of a vehicle hit by lightning? One thing she did remember was to make sure she jumped out of the truck with both feet leaving at the same time, right? The rubber on her tires was preventing the electricity from parting so she couldn't be touching the truck and the ground at the same time, right? If she did, she would be the lightning rod.

Adrenalin snapped through her and she grabbed the bag off the seat, popped open the driver's side and maneuvered herself so both her feet were firmly on the edge of the door opening. Wouldn't this just be great if she died of electrocution? And what if she was finally pregnant?

Emotions, thick and raw welled and she held back a sob. Her eyes blurred and she wanted to cry. Oh crap. What rotten luck. Maybe she should just sit here and wait for Max? Oh heck, he could be out there in the fields for hours. He always got lost in his work, especially during harvest time. She could call him on her cell phone.

Sighing in relief, she dug the cell out of her back pocket and hit the button to turn it on. Nothing happened.

"Oh, come on!" She hit the button several more times. Nothing. Dead battery? She'd just charged it a couple of days ago, for Pete's sakes!

Okay, so she was on her own. All she needed to do was jump and not touch any metal on the truck or touch the ground at the same time. She could do that. Simple. Yeah. Right.

And what if she was wrong about how to leave the truck? No, she wasn't. She had to be right.

She held her breath, stared at the ground. The ground was safety. Yeah, she was right. She had to be.

She didn't know how long she stood there, perched to jump. She prayed Max would come to her rescue. Even shouted into the eerily silent air a few times. He didn't come. Come to think of it, she didn't hear his tractor motor anymore either. Nor any birds singing. And what was with the wind? It was getting very cold.

Creepy weird.

Anxiety mounted. She felt sick to her stomach. Nausea. Distinctive and gut wrenching. Chills took hold and the frosty wind wrapping around her wasn't helping. Oh man, she was gonna be sick, if she didn't get out of this truck.

Teyla prayed. Hard. She prayed harder than she'd ever prayed. And then she jumped.

Nothing happened when she hit the ground.

Except she lost the contents of her breakfast. Bitter bile lurched out of her mouth and her stomach ached like a bitch. Her skin felt cold and clammy. Perspiration blistered over her forehead and under her arms.

The flu? Morning sickness?

Oh man, where was Max?

She shouted his name again into the deafening air. No answer. She made it into the house just in time to puke yet again into the kitchen sink.

If this was morning sickness, they could have it!

"It wasn't morning sickness. I miscarried that day and all I found left of my late husband was a pile of ashes drifting off his tractor seat." She felt cold and numb inside of her, saying it aloud. Just as she'd felt that day.

"I'm sorry. That was tough to go through. I'm really sorry," he whispered, and Teyla sighed as he caressed her hair.

She liked the feeling of him brushing her strands. It was soothing. Erotic. Nice. She sighed again and he squeezed his arms gently around her and for the first time ever, she relaxed in a client's arms.

"They say it had something to do with the solar flares targeting people that contained certain genes. Those people just evaporated. There wasn't anything you could have done for your baby, or your husband. It was just some freak science thing that no one saw coming. It was out of everybody's control. Totally out of your control," he whispered.

The tone of his voice was soothing and it just felt so normal to be lying here in his arms.

She'd lay here for just a moment, she thought to herself, then she'd get up and make him supper. But her eyelids grew so heavy. And she really liked listening to the steady way he breathed. He felt so warm and snug against her. She felt protected. Safe. She hadn't felt like this in a very long time. Too long to remember...

Logan knew the instant she fell asleep. Her body softened and melted against him. Her breathing slowed and her heart stopped hammering like crazy. Even now, after taking her, he wanted her again. There was vulnerability in her. A vulnerability he'd never seen before in the other professional women he'd slept with. An openness in her that brought out his protective side and suddenly he'd wanted to know where she'd been on that day that changed everyone's life forever.

While she'd relayed her story, he realized she wasn't bitter or hard. While they'd had sex, he'd also sensed she wasn't putting on an act. She hadn't faked her pleasure at his hands. He liked that. A lot.

Logan sighed and watched the strands of her hair move beneath his fingers as he caressed her. She had a really nice color of brown hair. In the twilight, he could see hints of gold and red twinkling there. And her hair felt so soft and silky as he stroked it.

She shouldn't be living out here all alone. Didn't she realize how dangerous the world had become? She needed a man to settle here.

A man to protect her from guys like him. Guys that wanted to take advantage of a woman living alone. A guy who wanted to share her with his partners.

Logan smiled. Yeah, the other two men would like this woman. He'd make sure Cassidy and Spencer dished out lots of pleasure. She wouldn't be disappointed. Not at all.

Chapter Three

When Teyla awoke, she felt surprisingly refreshed. Her breasts, for the lack of a better word, felt ravenously used. Orally used, actually, and her pussy throbbed with a pleasant soreness. She'd fallen asleep wrapped in a stranger's arms feeling all safe and satisfied. But while she slept, he'd slipped out of bed and extinguished all but one of her oil lamps and tossed some more wood into the fireplace. As she stared into the semi-darkness, she heard him moving around in the kitchen.

He was being quiet about it. The soft plop of a coffee pot being placed onto the wood stove. The slow opening and closing of the cutlery drawer. The creek of the cupboard door opening where she kept her mugs and plates. The man was hungry, Teyla thought as she smiled into the darkness.

Just then her stomach grumbled. Her smile widened. Obviously, she was hungry too. Come to think of it, she felt famished.

Climbing off the bed, she slipped the negligee over her breasts and did up the buttons. Grabbing her robe off the bed post, she wrapped the soft pink terrycloth cocoon around her before tiptoeing across the wood plank floor to hesitate in the slightly open doorway.

Maybe she should just stay in bed? He could join her. He could make love to her again.

Teyla linked. Make love? God, had she totally lost her marbles? She was a sex object to him. Nothing more. And she needed to make sure he had half the money up front, as agreed. Yeah, sure it was a little late in checking, but hey, he'd been damned good in bed, nicely distracting from the norm. She should be paying him. She stifled a giggle at that thought.

"Would you like to join me for a cup of coffee?" His deep voice echoed into the bedroom making her tense and her cheeks flame with instant heat.

Shoot! He'd heard her.

"Um, sure. Just give me a minute." To get my red, irritatingly blushing cheeks under control, she added silently.

"How do you take it?" he called again.

"Black." Considering sugar and cream were extremely in short supply, she would leave what little she had for her guest. "Sugar is in the canister on the table and some cream is in the jar on the east windowsill."

She didn't hear him move, so she figured he took his coffee black as well. Placing her palms against her warm cheeks, she willed them to cool, ordered herself to calm down.

Taking deep, steadying breaths, she finally managed to regain a semblance of control. Well, she may as well go out there and make the man some supper.

Maybe he'd thank her with another scorching session of sex?

Teyla rolled her eyes and chastised herself for thinking that way. He would take her because he wanted to, not because he was thankful for a good meal.

Making sure the sash on her robe was nice and tight, she self-consciously clutched the lapels around her throat and stepped out of the bedroom into the adjoining kitchen. The buttery glow from an oil lamp on a nearby shelf splashed over him.

He sat at the table, facing her. He wore only his jeans, and as she entered the room, he smiled making her tummy do some really nice flip-flops. When she spotted a couple of cute dimples pop out on each if his cheeks, she almost moaned aloud from the erotic jolt slamming through her.

Gosh, he really did look hot!

He seemed genuinely glad to see her.

"Great coffee," he said as he poured some into another mug, he had sitting near him on the table. Her gaze latched onto his long fingers, and she shivered as she remembered how intensely he thrust them into her vagina.

"Come, stand over here," he said.

She noticed his look suddenly seemed glazed with heat.

Trembling, with an odd sense of anticipation, she went to him. She swallowed as he reached out and pulled on her robe sash.

It fell open.

"You won't need this," he whispered and slipped the robe off her shoulders. He let it drop with a whisper.

"Or this."

He began unbuttoning those dainty buttons on her negligee. His fingers fumbled from not being used to such a delicate task, despite that, he did it in record time. He lowered the negligee over her shoulders, past her elbows and cool air touched her breasts as they spilled free for him to see.

He inhaled softly as he studied them. They felt so unbelievably heavy and she ached for him to touch her.

"I guess you figured out I'm a breast man."

"Really? I hadn't noticed."

Oh, her cheeks were warming up again as he stared at her breasts. She noticed there was a breathless tone to her voice too. A throaty tone she'd never heard before, let alone had known existed.

"Yeah. Yours are perfect."

His grin widened and spirals of something unnameable shot through her. His gaze made her feel jittery and feverish at the same time. In a good way.

"Why no guy has taken you for himself is just unbelievable," he burst out and just kept staring.

Her brain told her not to get sucked in by his kind words. Clients said all kinds of things in the heat of action. In most cases, they were fantasizing about a woman in their own life. A woman that had died in the Catastrophe, or a woman they couldn't have or a girlfriend who didn't want to do anal or oral or wouldn't put out when they wanted.

She knew she was second choice. Didn't have a problem with that. At least not until now.

She wondered who Logan was fantasizing about, as he gazed at her breasts. Wondered who he envisioned he was touching as he reached out both his hands and feather brushed her nipples until they grew so hard, she almost had to clench her teeth from the agony of wanting them in his mouth. She inhaled with the delightful sensations, the erotic thoughts. Her heart hammered as he pushed back his chair and stood, his fingers leaving her nipples.

He gripped her chin with his hand and tilted her head upward. She knew she was reading way too much into the awesome quiver rippling through her as she saw the sparkle of appreciation shining in his dark eyes. Despite trying not to melt against him, she couldn't help but to do just that. She pushed her lower half against his torso, feeling the magnificent bulge of his cock press against her panty, the only thing she was left wearing.

In response, he gyrated his hips against her, the hard knot of his erection pressing firmly against her lower abdomen. She moaned softly at the surprisingly beautiful feelings zipping through her and moaned again as he lowered his mouth upon hers.

Before his lips touched hers, she smelled coffee, and then tasted it as his mouth powered over hers, making her legs go weak and all her nerve endings stand to attention.

Gosh, the man knew how to kiss. His lips were firm and demanding, encouraging every inch of her to become aware of him. She gasped as a flare of need snapped through her pussy. Before she could stop herself from physically and emotionally falling into the sensual abyss of pleasure, she was already curling her arms around his neck and pushing wantonly against him.

His lips demanded, and took her breath away, made her mindless. His sexy scent filled her nostrils teasing her senses and snapping a wildfire deep inside her pussy. When he forced his way past her lips and thrust his tongue into her mouth, exquisite shivers rushed through her all the way down to her toes.

His tongue twisted with hers. Touched. Mated. Worked dark magic as his lips made love to her mouth, leaving her dazed and overwhelmed with erotic sensations.

Abruptly, he broke the kiss and she cried out when her feet suddenly left the floor and he was lifting her by her waist, placing her ass first onto the kitchen table. Sliding his warm hands between her knees, he opened her legs to him. She moaned as a finger slid into the opening of her panty and into her wet vagina. The onslaught of sensations from his penetration made her wonderfully off balance. She reached out and grabbed hold of a solid pair of shoulders.

"Say my name," he whispered as she panted.

"Logan," she breathed, loving the way his name rolled out of her mouth. Loving the intense way he studied her and the erotic way he withdrew his finger and thrust two into her pussy, this time with his knuckles massaging her clit as he slipped in, making want pound through every inch of her.

"Again," he commanded in a thick voice.

"Logan."

Her slick vagina clenched around his finger. She loved being impaled in this way, enjoyed the sensations exploding inside her every time he entered.

He kept pumping, this time with three fingers and leaned over, his head dipping, his succulent mouth latching onto her left nipple. Teeth tormented her tender bud as his fingers seduced her pussy. She gasped as an orgasm began to build. Closed her eyes to allow the climax to embrace her.

As if sensing she was nearing her climax, he let go of her nipple, withdrew his fingers. Grabbing her waist, he lifted her off the table, her knees almost buckling as she stood in front of him.

The sound of foil crinkling had her looking down as he ripped open a package. From the corner of her eye, she noticed on the table, beside his coffee mug, several condoms that he must have slipped out of the package in her room. She also saw the feed bag and money peeking out. She hadn't noticed them when she'd come in. Why hadn't she noticed? Because she'd been fixated on him, that's why. He seemed to be a magnet to her. A wicked distraction. A welcome change.

Hunger raced through her as drew her attention downward again and watched him roll on the condom. His cock appeared flushed and swollen and *very* erect.

Oh baby, come on give it to me. Just like before. This time, she didn't even try to chastise herself for wanting him or curse herself for allowing him to kiss her again.

Gosh, was she desperate for sex or was she desperate? She whimpered as he suddenly dropped to his knees before her. Staring down at him, she watched him slip his fingers beneath the waistband of her panty and slid the flimsy piece of material over her hips and down her legs. She stepped out of them and he tossed it beneath the kitchen table. He pressed his palms between her thighs, widening her legs some more.

"I noticed food is scarce around here," he commented as he suddenly looked up at her, his eyes laden with lust.

She nodded numbly, unable to grasp why he was talking about food when they both so obviously needed sex.

"I have something you'll like out in my satchel in the barn. I'm hungry, but I'm hungrier for you."

Oh God.

She inhaled sharply as he licked his lips and lowered his head to between her thighs. Yelped as his tongue slid between her pussy lips and he lapped her ultra-sensitive clit.

"I couldn't get enough of smelling you earlier. Need to taste you again," he said as he drew away and then went in with his head again.

She undulated as he licked her pussy again, his powerful tongue turning into an erotic whip as he lashed her clit. Exquisite pleasure rushed through her. He held her hips tightly so she could barely move and literally ate her vagina. The heat of his lips fused over her pussy and he sucked so hard she instantly exploded.

Shuddering waves ripped her apart. He devoured her. Tormented her. She fought to breathe as emotions and pleasure shot through her like a wanton tornado.

"Perfect," he gasped as he let go of her. He rose quickly, got into position in front of her and she whimpered as his thick cock head pressed between her labia folds. Clutching his biceps, she clenched her teeth as he worked his thick cock into her. Oh, God, had he been this big last time? Unbelievable pressure pillaged her as her vagina muscles stretched and gave way accepting the huge intruder. He withdrew, and as he thrust into her again, he took her mouth in another plundering kiss that rocked her to her very core.

He stroked his cock into her. Entering her with long thrusts that were strong and pushed her toward a climax.

He was so big inside her. She could feel every inch of him now, where their first time had been so frenzied and quick, she'd just let the sensations whipped through her. Now, he was taking his time, making sure she was feeling him. Feeling the heady kiss and the long torturously slow thrusts.

He began to pump harder, and she knew he must be feeling the power steamrolling toward them. He thrust his tongue into her mouth, matching the desperate thrusts of his cock.

And then Teyla was there.

Ecstasy. It burst through her with a white-hot lightning speed. Her thoughts melted and she became one with him, their bodies fusing, convulsing.

He swept her soul away, stripped her emotions bare with his driving strokes and when her orgasm was finally over, the spasms in her vagina ebbed away as they held onto each other.

She listened to his heavy breathing, committed the sound to her memory, knowing she wanted to keep every intimate detail of him in her mind so she could unbury them after he was gone. Unbury them during the long cold nights she spent alone.

"I'm going out to the barn and get some food," he said as he finally pulled out of her. She watched him tie off the condom and toss it into the wastebasket she kept in her kitchen.

"Get dressed. I'll be back in a few minutes," he ordered.

She made a move to bend over and retrieve the negligee, but he stopped her.

"There is another package in there." He nodded to a saddlebag slung over the back seat of another chair.

"Put what's in there, on. Leave the robe off."

She nodded and numbly watched him stroll to the side door, where he slid his big bare feet into his boots. Grabbing a sweater he'd left on the hook, he swept it over his glistening tanned body and then donned his leather jacket.

Without a backward glance, he opened the door and then the screen door. Stepping outside he shut the door behind him. The sound of it felt like a door closing on her heart. Sadly, reality rushed in and bitter tears swept into her eyes.

For a moment he'd made her feel. Made her remember what it felt like to be loved again.

Dammit! Why had she allowed him to kiss her? To allow him into her heart so easily? She was an object to him. Nothing more. What had she expected him to do anyway? Look back at her and say "See you later, my love? Or I'll miss you while I'm gone?"

Gosh, she was so pathetic. Why was she reacting so emotionally? What in the world, had she gotten into with this guy?

Stepping onto the porch, Logan moved quickly avoiding the miniscule buttery glow of lamplight splashing from the kitchen windows. Settling in the shadows, he waited several minutes, allowing his eyes to adjust to the darkness. Skimming the dark prairie horizon, he checked for any kind of movement and saw nothing.

No one, but he and that lady Dr. knew he was here. His partners would find out tonight or in the morning when they visited her and he'd instructed her to send them over tomorrow.

The doctor had been recommended by others in the gang he rode with. They said she was a woman known for treating injuries and not asking questions. Obviously, she took her doctor oath seriously and treated everyone the same. They said she was trustworthy.

Despite their reassurances, he couldn't shed the wariness of the hunted. He'd lived this way for a couple of years now and his instincts of being careful and alert had kept him alive. His instincts also confirmed that after meeting her, Dr. Liz could be trusted. Nonetheless it didn't hurt to be careful. He'd just stay here in the shadows for a couple of more minutes keeping an eye out.

He'd be lying if he denied he hadn't been turned on when the woman doctor had touched his balls and cock while examining him. According to the other members of the gang, anyone in this area who wished to purchase a clean pleasure girl for the evening went through Dr. Elizabeth Brandywine. Getting a clean bill of health had been worth it because she'd sent him here to Teyla. He was damned glad too that when Spencer, Cassidy and himself had picked straws, he'd been the one who'd picked the short straw between the three of them, allowing him to check out the prostitute first.

Whenever the gang did a job and broke up for safety reasons, he rode with his two friends. The three of them enjoyed sharing a woman. They also took turns in going to one first. The other two would take baths in a nearby town and get drunk. Celebrate the success of their latest job. Spend some of the stolen money. He was glad they'd screwed Baron again. Screwed him in his big fat pocketbook right where it hurt him the most.

Logan smiled as the sweet feeling of satisfaction purred through him at the thought of Moneybags Baron, as they liked to call the rich pudgy man, getting word that the Durango gang had taken out his train payload. Again.

Despite outrunning the posse that had been on their tail for over a week, they'd split the Durango gang into three groups. His trio had come across the state line into Canada and managed to give the posse the slip a couple of nights ago when they'd hit the Bow River.

The success of the job had been cause for celebration and he'd get drunk, but first he wanted Teyla again. Yeah, he'd really enjoy taking her again. Her cream was hot and delicious as it flowed into his mouth. Her scent sensual and arousing.

Man, and the hot way she moaned when he thrust into her, well, she just made him crave her bad. So bad that he wanted to take her into his arms every time he was near her.

A sudden urge to hurry out to the barn and get the grub prompted him to shift his ass into gear. Withdrawing his gun from where he'd left it in his leather jacket pocket as per Teyla's request he leave any weapons in the kitchen; he quickly crossed the yard toward the barn. He wasn't expecting any trouble as he'd done a good job covering his tracks from the Docs place. But he always liked to keep a gun handy, just in case.

As he neared the barn, the urge hit him to go around back to the greenhouse where she'd been working all day. There was a nip of frost in the air, and he wondered how her plants fared in this daily cold environment, due to the Catastrophe but then he stopped himself short.

Her greenhouse and her plants were no concern of his.

She was a pleasure girl. A woman to be used for his pleasure and then he'd ride out and never look back. Just like he'd done with the other ladies of the evening he'd been with.

But this time, the idea of simply riding out and leaving this woman behind didn't sit well with him. Cursing himself, he bypassed the barn and headed for that greenhouse.

Chapter Four

Teyla was trembling as she placed the chopped carrots and cubed potatoes into the boiling water of the pot sitting on her solar operated stove. Thanks to the solar panels on the roof of her farmhouse, she'd been able to have access to hot water, stove, and a bath, simply by switching over batteries when one was drained.

It had been her husband's idea when they'd first moved in several years before the Catastrophe had struck. Being in such a rural place with frequent violent snowstorms in the winter and thunderstorms in the summer, the backup solar energy when the electricity went out came in handy. Neither of them had anticipated exactly how good that idea would be until the electrical grids across the entire world fried during those solar flares.

Last she'd heard it would take years before her farm would be hooked to the grid again.

Until then, she could only hope the solar parts she had on hand, wouldn't break on her. Solar parts were very expensive on the markets.

Any type of light making such as candles, matches, oil lamps, gas lamps or any heat creation items such as wood stoves and pellet stoves could cost too much. She was lucky she had a cast iron wood burning stove in the kitchen as well as fireplaces in each of the bedrooms of her century old farmhouse. Speaking of fireplaces and wood stoves, she'd tossed even more wood onto the fire crackling in their bedroom; no correct that, her bedroom, as well as shoving more wood into the cast-iron stove, so it was nice and toasty in here.

She'd also checked his saddlebag. The one he'd slung over the back of the chair and had been surprised at the arrangement of knives, guns, and ammo he kept in there. Way too much for somebody just passing through. But it was none of her business, she told herself, reminding herself that Dr. Liz had sent him, so he would be fine.

So, she'd brought the money he'd had in the feed sack downstairs to the basement and hid it in the fruit cellar behind a shelf. She'd quickly checked the amount and it was exactly half the amount, as he'd said. Having that much money in her hands, in her basement, caused her to be nervous. It was just too good to be true. Great sex and getting paid for it. Amazing.

She'd also dressed in the clothing he'd indicated in that package. The negligee was similar in style to the other one, except this one was black, the skirt part being quite short revealing the thin panty she wore underneath. A panty, which also had a wide opening so he would have easy access to her.

She worried her lip and gazed down at herself, whimpering as she caught sight of her bare breasts sticking out seductively through the openings. She'd been stunned to discover he wanted her to wear such a provocative garment. But after her initial reaction, her pussy had clenched with such a desperate need to have him buried deep inside of her again that she'd been surprised at enjoying the erotic sensations shimmering through her at the thought of Logan gazing upon her breasts while she wore something he'd picked out.

She couldn't believe how easily he'd taken control of her body. Couldn't understand why she wanted him back in here with her so badly.

Was it loneliness? Had she been living out here by herself for too long?

It hadn't bothered her too much. She'd always been a bit of a loner, preferring her own company to others. Her husband had been the exception. He'd been the same as her. An introvert like herself.

They'd been true nerds interested in farming the old fashion way and creating organic foods for their community. That's how she still made some of her income. Growing organic food in her greenhouse out back. Not that people cared if the food was organic or not these days. Empty bellies made people desperate and they accepted all kinds of crap on the market.

But she'd managed to keep her vegetables clean and her prices from skyrocketing, refusing to take advantage of the desperation that was so rampant nowadays.

During her last trip to town a few weeks ago, the last her horse had taken before he'd died of old age, she'd heard that in some cities people were turning cannibalistic out of desperation for meat. They were reverting to kidnapping people off the streets, killing them and cooking, preserving them and even selling them as meat.

Teyla forced those horrid thoughts away. She preferred to live in her own fantasy world out here. Beyond her property was none of her concern. It was better this way. It kept her nerves intact. Nerves, which unfortunately, weren't quite intact at remembering Logan saying he wanted the agreement to include her having sex with his friends.

A wave of anguish washed over her. Three men? Oh lord. How would she be able to handle that? Would she be embarrassed or react as she had with Logan? Easily succumbing to pleasure. She'd never given up total control to a client before. To the pleasures.

At the sound of his boots on the steps outside, she resisted the impulse to dash over to the chair where she'd lain her robe over the back. No, she wouldn't hide herself from him.

He was her client. He was paying for her services. She was glad she'd applied some more delicate perfume on her wrists. It would cover the scent of her arousal. At least she hoped so. She didn't want him knowing how hot she was for him. She needed to keep things strictly professional.

She felt anything but professional as the door creaked open. God help her, she couldn't stop herself from glancing over her shoulder and gasp at the erotic sensations wrapping around her like a seductive glove when she caught sight of how wide his shoulders were as he stepped inside the kitchen his arms laden with a pile of firewood. Kicking the door shut behind him, he stopped when he caught sight of her watching him. His dark eyes literally glowed with appreciation.

"Turn around." he instructed.

His voice sounded thick and aroused and when she did as he asked and turned to face him, his gaze zeroed in on her exposed breasts. Her pussy creamed at the carnal look of promise flickering across his face.

"Put on your robe. I'll take you later. After we eat."

She creamed at his words. *I'll take you later.*

Gosh, what was her problem with this guy? First, he wanted her robe off, now on.

Grabbing her robe, she slipped it on and returned to her chopping and trying to ignore how small her kitchen suddenly seemed with him in it. He placed the firewood down on top of the current pile before heading back out the door again without so much as an explanation. She was thankful for his disappearance for it gave her a moment to catch her breath. And she meant that quite literally.

The scorching way he made her feel, when his gaze had dropped to her bare breasts lit a fierce fire of need coursing inside her. It was insane, the sexy way he made her feel. Everything about this client was so wrong. She didn't mean there was anything wrong with him. She meant what she was feeling for him was wrong.

She shouldn't be anticipating their next sex session with such enthusiasm. Why wasn't she embarrassed at wearing these revealing clothes he'd told her to wear? Why was she so easily following all his instructions without a second thought?

Because he's your client. That's what he pays you for, stupid.

She should be going up to him, unbuckling his pants, teasing him, playing the part of the prostitute, and reaching inside his pants and keeping him aroused. She should be all over him like she forced herself to do with the other men she entertained. Instead, she was letting him pleasure her. Making him supper. Like a domesticated wife.

Teyla blinked as a sudden roar of surprise washed over her. She hadn't cooked anything for a man since her husband.

Okay. She was lonely. Apparently, that's what had to be going on, but why with this guy? Why Logan? With a man who was going to share her with his two buddies. Maybe it was some sort of forbidden fantasy syndrome.

Yeah. That's what it must be.

One thing she knew for sure, she was attracted to him because of his confidence. She'd never met a man who could so easily speak of sex, bring her such pleasure, or want to share her with other men. To her those traits were sexy. It spoke of confidence in his ability in the bedroom. No shyness. And yes, she had to be totally nuts to believe all this bullshit she was telling herself. But believe it she did.

He returned a few moments later with a saddlebag slung over his shoulder. He looked like a biker cowboy minus the cowboy hat. His leather jacket creaked as he lifted the worn black leather saddle off his shoulder and plopped it on the kitchen table.

"I've got salted bacon. Throw it into whatever you're making," he said as he withdrew a pink paper wrapped package the size of a shoebox and tossed it onto the counter near her. "I got it at the butcher shop that just opened up in the nearest town. The bacon is salted and smoked. Should last you a few months if you go easy on it. Don't share it with any of your customers. It's for you only."

Emotions thick and raw welled, tightening Teyla's throat. No one had given her such an extravagant gift.

She accepted the item without a word. Not that she could say anything at the moment anyway. From its weight alone, she bet the bacon must have cost him a small fortune, and she simply could not believe her luck.

With shaking fingers, she unwrapped the package and her mouth watered at the succulent looking choice cuts. She'd never been a vegetarian type and had always enjoyed her meat, being raised on a cattle farm before marrying. She appreciated the work involved in raising animals for food. The Catastrophe had made the price of meat skyrocket and Teyla couldn't remember the last time she'd had store bought meat, let alone bacon.

Tonight's supper, no doubt would be a feast. She could almost taste the salty meat melting over her tongue and it looked so fresh and healthy. Removing several precut slabs, she chopped them and placed them into the boiling water.

Gosh, she felt like a queen tonight. A man had sexually satisfied her twice with the promise of more to come, plus decent meat for supper.

The scrape of the chair indicated he was sitting down at the kitchen table, and she could feel his scorching gaze watching her as she rewrapped the rest of the meat. She'd place it in the fruit cellar later.

"Did you count the money? Make sure it was all there?" he asked in a teasing tone, obviously noting his money had disappeared.

"Is there a reason why I can't trust you?" she asked as she shook some store-bought pepper and herbs from her greenhouse into the soup.

With the bacon she probably didn't need any salt. Besides, salt cost just as much as meat. She'd taste the soup a bit later when the meat was thoroughly boiled and add some if needed.

"You never did give me an answer regarding bondage."

"I didn't?" She answered a bit too quickly, and a bit too breathlessly. The question had caught her off guard and she felt flustered.

"No, you didn't," he said firmly.

No, she guessed she hadn't. That he would bring up the subject again and not force bondage on her said something about this guy, didn't it?

"And if I said only with you?" God, had she said that aloud?

"Then I'd say just with me."

She nodded, not knowing if she was acknowledging what he said, or if she was agreeing to it. Her cheeks grew quite toasty. It had to be from the steam wafting out of the soup, right?

"Exactly what would you do?" She had to be crazy asking him that question, but the curiosity of what he would do to her burned through her.

"Why don't you look at me when you ask me that question, Teyla?" His voice had dropped to a quiet tone. Quiet, yet oh so bold. Gosh why did he have to be so bold?

"I need to cut up some more bacon and get the table set. And so many other things..."

The squeak of his chair had heard tensing and blushing furiously. When his hands slid around her waist like two sizzling brands and his hard body pressed against her backside, that big knot of his arousal pushing against the crack of her ass, Teyla's breath caught.

He ground into her gently, his pressure whipping an excited frenzy through her, making her cream. He nuzzled his face against the juncture of her neck and shoulder and the raspy feel of his unshaven whiskers brushing against her delicate skin sent delightful shivers racing up and down her back.

"What would you like me to do to you, Teyla? Would you like me to bind your breasts? Tie them up until your flesh is so swollen and plump and I'm sucking your nipples so hard you'll be coming from those sensations alone."

Teyla swallowed at the sudden dryness in her mouth. Could a woman come, just like that? With him, probably, she acknowledged.

"Or maybe you'd prefer it if you were lying naked forward over the armchair of the living room couch? Your arms bound behind your back. Your legs spread eagle and tied apart. Your ass and pussy bare and vulnerable while three of us take turns with you? Our cocks thrusting and plunging into your pussy or ass over and over until you're screaming and begging for release? How's that sound, baby?"

Teyla cleared her throat and tried really hard to stay focused and not allow his soft voice to lure her into his world of bondage.

"Or would you rather have the three of us surprise you with something dark and naughty?"

He was still grinding his erection against her ass, and now he was kissing her earlobe, and sucking on it much in the same manner as he'd done with her nipples earlier in bed. Sucking and drawing on her flesh with confident erotic pulls that had her pussy pulsing and the area between her thighs soaking wet.

"I think I'd like the surprise," she whispered, loving the sexy way he made her feel and the scorching way he rubbed up against her.

He tensed ever so slightly, obviously surprised at her sudden submissive agreement.

"I think you'll be pleasurably surprised," he replied, nuzzling her neck some more. "Keep going. I'll just stay here and watch you work on supper."

Have mercy, with him touching her like this she could barely concentrate as she cut some more pieces of bacon.

"Um, could you pass me that frying pan?" She asked hesitantly, not wanting to break the erotic contact of getting out of his arms.

Holding her against him, he pulled the pan from the counter and tugged it over onto one of the burners. She turned on the burner and placed the bacon into the frying pan.

"I'm going to whip up some hash browns and bacon. I'm sorry if that's not enough, but it's all I've got until the soup is ready."

"Maybe you got all I need." He nuzzled his hot moist mouth against the juncture of her shoulder blade and neck making curious tingles flare through her. Oh, she liked this feeling. Having a man snuggling against her, having his strong hard body envelope her, making her feel safe.

"I'm afraid all I have to drink for us is water," she whispered, trying hard not to get too distracted with his cuddling.

Running some water in the sink, she quickly washed her hands. Reaching for her cutting board nearby, she brought it closer to her so she could cube some potatoes.

"The whiskey I brought into your bedroom will do."

"I'd appreciate it if you didn't get drunk." That was one thing, she was adamant about. Another pleasure worker she knew had had the misfortune of allowing her clients to drink. At one point she'd been servicing several men at the same time and they'd gotten too drunk. Things got out of hand and the worker had been viciously beaten and raped repeatedly over a span of several days. And now the woman didn't go near men. Teyla didn't want something so horrific happening to her.

"I like a little whiskey with my woman, but I promise I won't get drunk." He slid his hands off her waist and found the sash on her robe. Untying it, he slid the sash out of the loops. Uneasiness snapped into her. Was he going to strangle her with it?

For one horrible moment she realized exactly how vulnerable her work was. Entertaining men who could kill her by simply snapping of her neck. To her surprise he brought the robe sash down in front of her open robe. Looping the belt beneath her bared breasts, he then brought both ends up behind her neck, the sash lifting her breasts, making her very aware of them as he tied the sash behind her neck.

"How does it feel?"

It felt amazing actually. This new position made her breasts stick out more and made them feel tighter.

"Umm... different," she confessed.

She couldn't help but gasp as he cupped her breasts, his hands holding her flesh, while his thumbs erotically brushed across the tips of her nipples.

"Umm...I...can't cook with you doing this," she admitted. The knife loosened in her palm.

"Don't worry; you're cooking up a storm."

He nuzzled his face between the strands of her hair and kissed the back of her neck. She lost all concentration and dropped the paring knife.

"Just ignore me," he whispered, his warm breath sending red hot tingles shooting through her.

"Kind of hard," she mumbled, but managed to grab the paring knife again and struggled to finish cubing the potatoes.

"Your breasts feel truly amazing," he breathed as continued to cup them while she stirred the bacon and tried hard not to submit to the molten desires he invoked with his caresses.

"What you're doing feels amazing," she acknowledged.

"Good. I'm because I am actually seducing you."

No shit, Batman.

"You're succeeding."

"How so?" He returned to nibble on her other earlobe.

"I want to have sex with you again." Her cheeks burned at her admission. He must think she was some inexperienced chick at the way she kept blushing around him.

"And I with you. But first we need to eat. I plan on working you again, so you'll need your strength."

Oh my. He certainly did have a way with words. "You better put those potatoes into the pan before the bacon burns."

Teyla blew out a tense breath, and while his hands caressed her breasts and his calloused thumbs brushed her nipples, she barely managed to get the potatoes into the frying pan.

"I bet you are nice and wet for me, aren't you?" he asked.

Wet is an understatement, mister. And why didn't he check? She found herself lying back against him, her body melting into his hardness.

"Was wondering when you'd loosen up," he chuckled against her ear.

Loosen up? Was he serious? She couldn't get any tenser.

"Where are the dishes? I'll set the table." There was hesitation in the way he unfolded himself from her and she wanted him back pressing against her. Wanted him wrapping his arms around her, his cock pushing into her ass. His hands cupping her.

She swallowed and cleared her throat and took her mind off those intimate thoughts.

"Up there. In the cupboard."

Gosh, she felt shaky. She bet he could hear it in her voice too. And yes, he was right, she thought as he opened the cupboard and dragged out two plates. She was so wet and her pussy felt so unbelievably swollen. She didn't think she'd felt so turned on before, ever.

He grabbed some forks and knives from a drawer, plus a couple of glasses from another nearby cupboard and set the table. A moment later he disappeared from the kitchen and she knew he'd retreated to the bedroom for the whiskey bottle. She wished she could touch her pussy and bring herself off. She swore she was steaming down there and her breasts weren't any better off.

She dared to look down and gasped at the fullness of her breasts. Her nipples were red and throbbed painfully against the material of her robe as she tugged it closed.

"Leave it open. I want to watch them while we eat."

A funny spasm zipped through her pussy at his words and she watched him come into the room with the whiskey bottle in his hand. Involuntarily, she let out a little whimper. It was a sexual sound. Aroused and full of heat.

"Don't worry baby. I'll bring you the relief you're craving. Just remember that good things come to those who wait."

She didn't say anything. Heck couldn't think of anything to say, as she lifted the frying pan, turned off the stove and prayed she had enough strength in her legs to carry the rest of the way to the table.

"We can eat this. I expect the soup will be done in about an hour," she said as she dished out the crisp bacon and steaming potatoes. Her mouth watered at the tangy scent of the dish.

"We won't be having soup tonight," he replied as he poured them both a healthy shot of whiskey. He trapped her gaze with his and she saw the dark look promise more pleasure.

Boy. Oh boy. Oh boy. She could only hope his two friends were going to make her feel this good when they showed up tomorrow.

The bacon tasted better than she ever thought it would, and so did the potatoes. The saltiness of the meat exploded over her taste buds and she found herself thinking this must be how it felt for her tongue to have an orgasm.

"What's got you all smiling?" he asked as he quickly shoved forkfuls of food into his mouth. The man was enjoying his meal and that made her feel really good.

"Tastes good. Thanks for the bacon," she said.

He smiled around the fork and once again her belly did the awesome fluttery flip.

"Thanks for the sex," he replied, and his smile got even bigger as he wolfed down another forkful.

Okay, her cheeks were heating up yet again, and so was she as his scorching gaze dropped to the area where the robe had been left open as per his request. He licked his lips and the sight of his tongue had her just about squirming in her chair wanting to squish her aching pussy against her seat in an attempt at some sort of release. God, he seemed like some sort of drug to her. And the exotic way he'd touched her had her wondering if he wanted her hooked on him.

"What are you thinking?" he asked, his gaze now back on her face. His eyes had a nice twinkle to them and she recognized it as curiosity.

"Well, I am wondering who you are. Where you come from?" she admitted. And why am I reacting so much to you? She silently added.

He shrugged his shoulders and frowned, giving her the impression, he didn't like her question. Well tough.

"I am a man who comes from here and there."

"Hmm, here and there and everywhere, right?"

He winked in answer and helped himself to more bacon and potatoes.

"What kind of work do you do?" she asked.

"Let's just say I'm a traveling salesman and leave it at that."

"A seller of bacon, no doubt."

He grinned. "No doubt."

"Mystery man."

"It keeps the ladies curious and interested."

I'm sure, she thought silently. A fissure of jealousy at the thought of him being with other women reared its ugly head. Suddenly she needed to know this man. Needed to peel away the layers of mystery he hid behind.

"Where were you when *it* happened?" She asked.

By the way his shoulders tensed and the fork full of food halted midway to his mouth he knew what she meant. She also realized her mistake. Never ask personal questions of your clients. It helped keep the relationship strictly professional and kept an emotional barrier between them. But she realized she'd never wanted so badly to crash through that wall he'd just erected.

"Let's say it was a bad day for everyone and leave it at that."

She nodded jerkily, but questions began to form in her mind. Did he have a wife? Girlfriend? Kids? He had to be around her age. Maybe he had had a family and they all died? Just like hers had died. All turning to ash or dust or whatever one called it when one simply self-combusted.

Remembering how she'd found dust on her parents' kitchen chairs when she'd gone searching for them made the bacon and potatoes, she'd been chewing turn into a flavorless cloth. She struggled to swallow it. Left the rest on her plate. Best not think about family. Best to live in the present. He was right. It was best to leave it.

He continued eating, his watchful gaze on her, but he remained silent. That is until he finished.

"I've got something that'll cheer you up."

He pulled his saddlebag closer, reached in and to her surprise and delight he pulled out a tin of peaches.

"Oh my God. They're making canned fruit again?" She asked as she took the heavy tin into her hands and read the paper pasted to it. *Made in Florida*. No way! She'd heard that Florida was a cold place now and all the citrus trees had frozen and died.

"Actually, no I picked it up a few days ago. It was made before the Catastrophe but I'm told it's still good. Shall we find out?"

Teyla nodded and he produced a can opener from his bag. My, the man came well prepared, didn't he?

He chuckled. "Cost a pretty penny. Hell, I never thought a can of peaches would be worth the same amount of money that a car used to sell for before the catastrophe."

Alarm bells once again whispered through her head. Where did a man get so much money? Illegally was the only answer she could come up with. But how unlawful was illegal?

Who cared. Not her business where he got his money. He was her client and that was all that mattered. Right? Right, she firmly told herself. Not her business.

Her mouth watered as he lifted the lid and proceeded to divvy up the healthy-looking peaches. They were sliced just the way she liked them. In quarters. And her taste buds literally exploded as the sweetness of the peaches splashed around in her mouth as she chewed. Definitely, still good.

They both made sexy moans as they slowly savored the treat. Teyla was smart enough not to rush it, accepting the flavor, committing it to memory, knowing she may never have another chance at having canned peaches again. At the very least, not for a very long time.

They both tipped their plates and allowed the remaining juices from the peaches to slide into their mouths. She made sure to lick her plate too, savoring the sweetness. When they were both finished, he gazed at her untouched glass half full of whiskey.

"How about shooting down your whiskey, and then we can take a nice walk outside."

His suggestion of a walk both disappointed and excited her. Having the peaches had chased away the sad memories of the past and brought back the need for more sizzling sex with him. Taking a walk in the dark had been something she hadn't done in quite some time. The dark spooked her but taking a walk with Logan sounded genuinely nice.

"As long as I can wear some warm clothes," she teased.

"The minute we come back, I want those clothes off," he commanded in a hoarse voice.

"Only if yours come off too. I'll drink the whiskey when we come back."

He nodded. "Okay, get dressed and hurry or I just might take you right here again."

She wanted to tell him that's what she wanted but he was already heading to the hook where he'd left his leather jacket. As he zipped it up, he saw her watching him and chuckled for her to get a move on.

Minutes later, she'd put on a pair of jeans, snug wool socks, a warm pink sweater, and her burgundy cardigan. Giving her hair a quick brush, she enjoyed the look of appreciation in Logan's eyes when she joined him at the kitchen door. Stuffing her feet into a pair of her late husband's warm work boots she followed Logan out the door and into the darkness.

Frosty air snapped against her face and hands as she locked the door. She didn't expect anyone to be around out here but having all that money in her basement called for some sort of security. Sliding the key into her cardigan pocket, she turned around and realized it wasn't actually that dark.

The sky literally danced with white and green moving lights. She'd heard the light had something to do with the magnetic layers surrounding the Earth's atmosphere being disturbed since the solar flares. That was another reason the climate had gotten colder since then. A mini Ice Age, they said, was happening on the other side of the earth. Surviving scientists couldn't agree if the Ice Age would eventually encompass the entire earth or if things would stay the same or get warmer someday.

She followed him down the stairs and they walked along the dirt road that wound through her property. The walked side by side for a long time in the stillness and she really felt safe having him here. Gone was the feeling that every shadow was a murderer and every sound a pack of wild dogs sneaking up to rip out her throat.

"I want to apologize for my earlier behavior," his deep voice burst through the quiet night air like a thunderclap shaking her feelings of security.

Earlier behavior? Until now, he'd been quite the gentleman. Had she missed something?

"You asked me where I'd been during the Catastrophe and I gave you the brush off."

"It's my fault," she said trying to reassure him. "It's none of my business."

He gave her a weak smile. "If you can talk about it with me, a complete stranger, I should do the same. I owe you that much."

"You don't own me any explanation."

"I had a wife and two daughters," he said quietly and she immediately detected the pain in his voice.

"You don't have to-"

His gaze snapped to her face and his eyes softened.

"I know. I want to. I figure it's as good a time as any. And I'll have you to drown my sorrows in after."

She swallowed and waited.

"I was with my daughters when *it* happened. We'd gone on our annual dad-daughters camping trip. My wife hated camping, so she always stayed home. But my girls..." his voice thickened with emotion.

"How old were they?"

"Jenny was twelve. Lynn was eleven. They loved to go to a new camping place every year. So, this time around, we decided on a group of caves two days drive from home. We were going to make it a weeklong trip. We were actually inside the caves when it happened."

Horror raced through her. He must have seen them disintegrate.

"We had no idea anything was wrong until we returned to the campground and realized there weren't any people around."

Relief swept through her. "The girls survived the solar flares."

He nodded. "My daughters survived the Catastrophe. I wish they hadn't. It would have been a much easier death."

Uneasiness snapped through her. Obviously, his kids had died.

"I couldn't get the car started, couldn't find a soul to help. Not one person. It was eerie, and I could tell the girls were getting uneasy. There was nothing but static when we tried to use our cell phones. I knew something was seriously wrong when we went to the campground office and found the door unlocked, and no one but a whimpering dog who was lying beside a pile of what looked like ashes on the floor.

I thought maybe some nutcase was on the grounds and had maybe tried to build a fire indoors and everyone had been evacuated. That's when I also noticed there was no electricity. The coolers full of food and drinks weren't humming. The air conditioner wasn't going as had been the couple of times we'd gone in during the week and it was pretty warm inside the building. Things were just off; you know what I mean?"

Teyla nodded. Yes, she understood. All survivors understood the desolation they'd experienced after realizing something of cataclysmic proportions had happened.

"We found a car with a key in the ignition and piles of ash on the front seats and back seats. I sat on the ash, turned the ignition, nothing happened."

He sat on the ash. On a dead person.

"How did you get home?" She didn't have to ask if his wife had survived. She knew instinctively she hadn't.

"We stayed at the campsite that night. Realized we were totally alone. Realized something bad had happened. We spent the next day outfitting ourselves with knapsacks, filling them with non-perishable foods from the store. Bottled water. I had a gun and we found some hunting knives for the girls. My youngest, she wasn't handling it too well. Crying. We were worried about Ann."

Ann, his wife.

"We started walking. You know kids that age; they can't walk as long as an adult so after a few hours they were pretty tired. We noticed a farm with grazing horses. Helped ourselves to four of them and of course no one was around at the nearby farmhouse or barn. My oldest daughter had a passion for horses and knew all about saddles and bridles and what horses ate. Don't know what we would have done without her. She showed us how to ride and we followed the highways home. We saw no one. Just abandoned cars and trucks – ashes in them. I kind of got the idea they were people, disintegrated.

Checked out a couple of houses for more food. It was the same story. Unlocked doors. Pets going hungry. We left the doors open so they could get outside. We couldn't take them with us. When we got home, we found her in the bed. Nothing but a pile of ashes beneath the covers. She was probably taking an afternoon nap. She did that sometimes after working in the vegetable garden. We buried her out back and tried to make do the best we could."

"And your daughters?" She asked softly as they turned and headed back to her farmhouse.

"I made the mistake of leaving them home alone one day while I went foraging at some neighboring homes for more food. When I came back, they were both dead. Hung themselves in the basement."

Shock sliced through her. "Oh my God. I'm so sorry," she whispered.

He cleared his throat and it sounded thick with emotion. Understandably. She felt her own emotions welling too at the thought of how horribly shocking it would have been to find his two children hanging. It must have been so devastating.

"They wanted to be with their mother. Besides, I wouldn't want them growing up in this world. It's an evil dark land now. Every person for themselves. They would have grown into desperate human beings, doing things that they would normally never have had to do in the old world, just to survive. Just like the rest of us."

Just like the rest of us. Meaning he was doing something he would never have done in his life. Just as she was doing.

They both fell silent again as they walked. The glow lacing the sky lit their way, giving an eerie greenish view of her farmhouse and the outer buildings in the distance. She realized now that there really wasn't anything to be afraid of out here. Just her vivid imagination. She smiled at that thought and to her surprise Logan's hand laced with hers. He squeezed her fingers gently as if telling her everything was going to be alright and for the first time in a long time, she actually felt that, yeah, maybe things might work out okay, even if the weather did stay this way.

Chapter Five

"**D**o you think it'll ever go back to normal?"

Logan heard the hopefulness in her question. Knew she was talking about the cold weather. He also knew he should sugarcoat what he'd heard. Protect her from the truth. It would be better if someone else dashed her hopes. But maybe the truth would be better if it came from him.

"Nothing will ever be the same" he answered. May as well let her know what he'd heard. "They're saying it will probably take hundreds of years before the weather returns to normal. But look at the bright side; you'll have vegetables from your greenhouse so you'll never starve."

She chuckled in agreement. It was a nice sweet innocent sound he would like to hear more of.

"So, you enjoyed supper?" she asked timidly as they walked into the yard.

"Definitely. And I'm really going to love dessert."

She smiled shyly and his heart did a really neat flip. Yeah, he liked her. Liked her a lot.

"I thought the peaches were dessert," she replied.

He could hear her voice was a little husky. He knew she was teasing about the peaches because he also knew she understood what he was talking about. That he wanted more sex from her. She was dessert. He realized he probably would never get tired of her. She was too refreshing a woman for a man to be tired.

"I haven't had dessert yet," he replied.

He saw the little shiver of anticipation rock through her. Felt it simmering inside him too. Like a volcano ready to erupt.

Touching her breasts and cuddling with her earlier while she'd prepared supper had only stoked the fires within. He'd wanted to take her right then, but he knew he'd probably come across as a sex starved crazed lunatic. He certainly didn't want her to think that about him.

Okay, so he was sex starved but a lunatic? Well, maybe.

Any man who rode for the Durango gang had to have some loose screws. They were a Robin Hood type gang. Steal from the rich and give to the poor. Give to themselves first, as well as their own selected charities. The best part of his job was when they'd ride by a derelict house with people living there wearing nothing but soiled clothing and bawling hungry babies. They'd drop off some money on the porch or one of them would ride up to the lady of the house and hand her the money telling her to buy milk for the kids.

The women appreciated that, especially if they were alone with kids. Perhaps giving to the poor was to ease their conscience? Hell, he didn't care. Just as long as those rich bastards got screwed for taking advantage of people. He stifled the threat of the familiar red-hot anger that always came when he thought of those so-called capitalists who were jacking up the prices unnecessarily and re-focused his attention on Teyla.

"I haven't seen any signs of hired hands. Do you run your greenhouse and the land by yourself?" He didn't notice any tilled land, so he already knew the answer. But he just wanted to make sure she really was all alone out here.

"I run this place myself. I did have a horse until recently, but he died. Buried him over there on that hill beside my husband."

He followed to where she pointed off to the south and noticed a pond and behind it a small hill. Yeah, that would be the hubby who turned to ash. Just like millions of others during the Catastrophe.

He caught some tears sparkling in her eyes and he resisted the urge to put a comforting arm across her shoulders. *No emotions, my man. Those are the rules,* he chastised himself.

He would be here for only another day and a night and then he'd be gone, rejoining with the Durango Gang, and taking from the rich to give to the poor.

Yeah, he knew he was doing wrong. But hell, so were the rich guys. And he also knew two wrongs didn't make it right. One day he'd have to quit and make amends but maybe not for a very long time.

They walked up the stairs and she unlocked the door in silence. He resisted the urge to check around her home, just to make sure no one had slipped inside while they'd been out. Man, he needed to shrug off this feeling of being hunted or he wouldn't enjoy the rest of his time here with her. Making a conscious effort to pretend life was normal, he helped her off with her cardigan. He hung it up on a nearby hook, and then he got rid of his jacket too.

It was nice and warm in here compared to outside and as she walked toward the sink, he realized he didn't want her washing the dishes or doing any type of work, except being with him. He wanted her now. Bad.

Reaching out, he grabbed her arm and twirled her around. Her sweet mouth went into an o shape of surprise and he just couldn't resist her any longer. The minute he melted his mouth over hers, the intense need sliced through his system like an explosion. Since touching her earlier his cock had remained heavy and swollen, painfully erect pressing way too insistently against his prison tight jeans. Now all he wanted to do was get his clothes off and bury his aching cock inside her warmth.

As he kissed her deeper, he felt her palms slip against the back of his neck pressing him harder against her mouth.

Oh yeah, he liked this woman.

He plundered her lips. They were cool from outside and he tasted their dewy freshness. He drove his tongue into her willing mouth and loved the fact she accepted him with ease and eagerness. She moaned softly, the sound sexy and sultry, filled with need. He growled as her cool hands slid from his neck, her palms sliding erotically over his chest down to the clasp on his jeans. She popped it open and he heard the zipper lowering. His knees weakened with the fierce need rushing through his bloodstream, but he forced himself to grab her wrists. To stop her.

She whimpered as he broke the kiss and appreciation slammed through him at the pink pleasure washing her face. Her lips were red and swollen from his kiss, her eyes glazed with sexual heat. He saw the question in her look. The one that asked if she'd done something wrong and that's why he was stopping her.

"Not yet. I need to prepare you before we go any further. Prepare you for the others. For tomorrow."

Fear and excitement flared in her eyes. They warred for a few seconds and the excitement won.

"Go into the bedroom and get naked on the bed. I'll join you in a few minutes."

"You're torturing me here," she breathed, reluctantly leaving his arms, and doing as he instructed.

He liked that she followed his orders. Liked that she was so eager to climb into bed with him again.

Logan grinned. "That makes two of us."

When she entered the other room, he sighed heavily as the yearning to take her raged through him. Strolling to the woodstove, he seized a couple of split logs from the pile, opened the cast iron door and shoved the wood inside onto the flickering fire. Then he grabbed what he needed from his saddlebag and pocketed it. He lifted the pot of hot water steaming off the top of the stove and poured some into a nearby ceramic basin. He dashed the hot water with some cold water from a nearby bucket and dipped in his finger making sure it wasn't too hot.

Ensuring the door was locked; he noted she hadn't drunk the whiskey he'd poured earlier during supper. That was okay. Maybe she just wasn't the drinking kind of girl and realized she was a first.

He spiraled a finger around the neck of his whiskey bottle, positioned the lone oil lamp in his palm and grabbed the basin with water, then entered the bedroom. There was enough of a glow splashing from the lamp he held and from the fire glittering in the hearth that he could make her out sitting on the bed. Her lower half was covered beneath a comforter but her breasts were exposed. A shaft of desire ripped through him at the sight of her large suckable nipples.

Control my man. Control. You need to prepare her. Then you can take her as much as you want.

He ignored her and his throbbing cock as best as possible as he deposited the ceramic tub filled with warm water onto the dresser and headed into the adjoining bathroom.

Teyla's heart hammered a mile a minute as she listened to Logan rummaging around in her bathroom. What was he up to with the ceramic basin? Why was he in the bathroom again? When he reappeared in the doorway, her lower belly fluttered with appreciation at how wide his shoulders looked. She couldn't get over how wonderful she felt just gazing upon him and how it seemed as if she'd known him for like ever.

He strolled with confidence in his long strides as he walked toward the dresser. He appeared as if he wasn't in a hurry. As if he didn't have the same urgency running through him as she did.

Damn him. Why did he affect her so much? Why did she want him to be inside of her so badly? It was nerve-racking need she'd never experienced before.

Warily she watched as he placed a towel, lather brush and a bar of soap on top of the dresser. He took a swig from his whiskey bottle before dragging another throwaway razor from his pocket, thrusting off the plastic protective cap and then dousing the blade area with whiskey.

"Umm, did you want me to shave your face?" Surely, he didn't expect her to give him another shave down there.

"I'm going to do the shaving" he reassured her. His next words made her want to bolt. "On your pussy."

She swallowed as nervousness skittered through her.

"My..."

"The boys like their pussy nude," he interrupted. "You'll also be more sensitive toward the pleasure."

Oh, of course. For a brief moment she'd forgotten she was merely here to be their pleasure toy.

He frowned and looked at her kind of funny, but she plastered on a smile. One she suddenly didn't really feel. But she needed to remember her agreement with him. He could do what he wished and she was a pleasure girl. His wish was her command.

Her disappointment faded quickly as she watched him drop a face cloth in the steaming water. Having him shave her would be an interesting experience; she realized and tried hard to control her rapid breathing.

"Where did you want me?" She tried to inject a professional tone into her voice, but it came out breathy and low. Too sensual, dammit.

"Over here on the side of the bed. On the edge like last time. Legs up on the bed with your knees wide apart. While I shave you, I want you to play with your nipples. Want you ready for me when I take you."

She swallowed as his husky spoken words draped over her like velvet. Her lower belly clenched and her pussy quivered as she thrust the sheets off her. She got into the position, across the bed, then lay on her back, bringing her ass as close to him and the edge of the bed as possible before bringing her knees up and spreading her legs for him.

His gaze was smoldering as he looked between her thighs and licked his lower lip.

He nodded to her, "Play with yourself."

She bit her bottom lip and found her nipples. They were already hard and sensitive as she pinched and feathered them. Her breathing quickened even more as she reacted to her touches. His breaths also came faster and louder as he watched. His Adams apple bobbed as he swallowed and then he reached into the basin bringing out the steaming face cloth. He waited a moment; probably thinking it was too hot before he squeezed the cloth then lowered it over her pussy. Heat exploded against her flesh and she moaned at the intensity of the contact. He tucked the edges of the hot cloth in against the sides of her labia and went about lathering up the soap with the lathering brush.

He didn't say anything as he worked. But the slow and easy way he moved the lather brush loaded with frothy raspberry scented soap and then following up with the razor was in direct contrast to the quick way his eyes were darting first to her face to catch her gaze, then to watch her touching her breasts and then down to where he moved her labia this way or that while he worked on shaving her pussy.

When he finished cleaning away the soapy areas with water and the cloth, he finally spoke. "I want to prepare you now. For the others. Turn over onto your belly."

She nodded and sat up. She set a couple of pillows on the bed and then lay down on her stomach, angling her hips over the pillows.

She inhaled sharply as his warm palms smoothed over her ass cheeks. His fingers trailed along the crack and he hesitated when she tensed as he touched her tight sphincter.

"Easy, baby. Loosen up," he murmured.

She breathed harshly, tried to relax, and waited anxiously as he smoothed his palms once again over her ass cheeks. He was taking his time she realized. Calming her with his touch like a master would try to calm a frightened mare.

"Breathe deeply. Breathe slowly" he whispered. The gentle sound of his voice had her relaxing.

"Dr. Elizabeth said you've done anal before," he said a moment later.

"I have," she answered truthfully, feeling her cheeks heat. The couple of regulars who enjoyed anal had small cocks. Nothing compared to the size of Logan.

"The plugs I saw in the bathroom drawer aren't going to stretch you enough for my boys. I have a bigger one. Unused. No need to worry about that."

Arousal slashed through her. Her pussy creamed at the thought of his friends being as big as Logan.

To her surprise, he slapped her ass. Hard. Her skin stung and she gasped at the unexpected impact. He slapped her ass a few more times until her skin burned and she was gripping the comforter tightly against the hot blaze.

To tell the truth the erotic way he slapped her seemed caring compared to how the other guys she entertained did it. Erotic indeed and arousing.

"Nice and pink. I like a blushing ass. I can't wait to take you, Teyla. My cock is so hard and swollen just thinking about the boys watching me taking you in the rear."

Teyla swallowed at the visions his confession whipped up. Her tied to the bed while men took turns taking her ass. Oh boy, she shouldn't be thinking about this. Shouldn't be getting so excited. He was just a job. What he wanted was just her job. She shouldn't be anticipating the arrival of two more strangers as much as she was. It just wasn't normal.

His hands curved over her warm cheeks again and she couldn't help but move her buttocks against his palms as sweet need swept through her. Yes, she did want Logan to do her first. To give her the pleasure first. She blew out a long slow breath and held the comforters tighter.

A moment later he smoothed his hands away and she heard the sound of plastic ripping. It was followed by water tinkling in the basin. She angled her head so she could watch and caught glimpses of a huge black butt plug, one end tapered, and the shaft almost as thick as Logan's cock.

She creamed and trembled at the same time as a mixture of emotions charged through her. Nervousness, at not being able to relax enough to take the plug and excitement at how it would feel buried inside her. All her clients were average sized when it came to their cocks. The two who did anal were small, so she'd had little problem wearing the plugs she had. No problems taking their cocks inside her.

She always made it a habit to prepare herself with a plug a day or two before an anal regular came to visit. Maybe that's why she couldn't totally relax this time? Because of the unexpectedness of this stranger's arrival and the large size of the plug?

The sound of her lube jar, the one she kept on her dresser, opening, had her eyes widening. She watched his fingers dip into the jar. He came out with a generous amount and smeared it liberally over the tapered end of the plug.

His eyes looked dark with intent as his gaze moved from the plug to study her ass. Fire whipped through her and she could see the need pulsing through his eyes. Could feel it building through her too. He placed the plug down on the towel and she whimpered as his lubed finger touched her tight sphincter and he pushed past her protesting muscles. She heard him groan as her muscles gripped his fingers with wanton welcome.

His other lubed finger slipped against her clitoris and she gasped as he began a splendid massage that had her writhing. While he seduced her clit, a finger pushed deeper into her ass. The pressure of the entry had her breathing deeply as she struggled to relax. A second lubed finger entered her ass. She accepted him, her muscles eager and gripping. She moaned at the sensations, the pressure, and the wicked burn of entry.

It was quiet in here, in her bedroom. Quiet, except for the sounds of her soft moans and the squish of lube as he continued his seductive massage on her clit. She could feel the warm wetness pool between her thighs, the push toward oblivion. The bliss beyond reach.

Lubed fingers stretched deeper into her ass, explored, and caressed and then he began a gentle pumping motion. Every entry went deeper and she was shifting her hips on the pillows, widening her legs, needing a quicker, firmer pressure on her clit, a faster rhythm in her ass.

She whimpered as erotic sensations grabbed and took hold. He was pushing her toward an orgasm and then his voice split through the silence and pulled her back to reality.

"Easy baby, I don't want you to come yet."

No, please. Now. She wasn't sure if she said it out loud or not but she cried out in disappointment as he withdrew his fingers and he moved away.

"I'm putting in the plug next, baby. Just a bit more time and then I'll take you," he whispered in a hoarse voice.

Anticipation rocked her. He pulled her ass cheeks apart and she moaned as the lubed flared tip of the plug gently sank into her. Heat burned through her as the pressure built.

Oh my! It feels so big!

"I know you're not used to the size," he said gently. "This plug is almost as big as me and the boys."

The boys. She inhaled sharply at the thought of three men taking her tomorrow.

"Take some deep breaths, baby. It'll pinch then I'll make you feel better."

Her breaths sawed in and out as she fought to control them. Incredible pressure continued to build. Finally, the plug stopped, fully buried. The immense size felt odd lodged in her. Odd, but in a good way and she inhaled in relief.

"I have another surprise for you," he murmured. "But first I want you to stand beside the bed and wait for me to come back."

She nodded numbly and gasped as the thick plug wedged even deeper inside her as she stood. He disappeared into the kitchen, taking the basin of water with him.

"I know you're really wet for me, so I want you to play with your clit," he called out from the other room.

She could hear the rip of plastic, the splash of water and she wondered what he was up to next.

"Play gently," he called out. "Keep yourself humming for me. Don't bring yourself off. I will do that for you."

"O...okay," she managed to say in a breathy voice that sounded so not like hers.

Her legs were trembling as she stood, her pussy tight and needy, her inner thighs drenched with warm cream and the lube he'd used.

She stood in front of the mirror watching herself as she widened her legs. Panting, she touched her clit and watched her eyes flare with heat. Her cheeks were flushed and her eyes twinkled with a rare happiness.

Her heart beat madly as she gingerly massaged her clit and played with her nipples. She became so entranced watching herself she didn't hear Logan enter the bedroom until she smelled him. Then he was touching her backside with something and peered over her shoulder, catching her gaze in the mirror. She inhaled harshly at the lust written all over his face. Lust and raw need.

"I've got a thick dildo for you. I want to take you with it. Watch you come while I'm doing you."

Her pussy clenched. She bit her lower lip to keep from crying out as he instructed her to place her hands on the bureau, widen her legs more and stick out her butt.

His instructions were driving her wild. Obediently, she did what he told her to do and splayed her palms on top of the bureau feeling the cool smooth wood beneath her fingers as she waited. Then he disappeared from her view, and she realized he'd dropped to his knees behind her. She swallowed at the feel of the smooth head of the dildo lodged against her vaginal opening.

"Take it in, Teyla. Take it all the way in," he said softly as he slid the huge dildo slowly into her.

Because of the plug, her vagina was ultra-tight, and she fought to breathe as he withdrew and softly entered her again. And again. Going deeper into her with every erotic thrust. Her pussy muscles clenched and she could feel the elevated veins on the toy as she gripped it, sucking it into her. She moaned and whimpered as a stimulator pressed against her clit. Cried out as he withdrew and then plunged into her again. The dildo stretched her as she'd never been stretched before.

She gazed in the mirror. Watched her eyelids droop. Saw him standing there again behind her studying her while he thrust in and out until she was panting and gyrating her hips and loving the hard long thick dildo plunging in and out of her. Sensations burst through her, rocked her.

"Oh God!" She cried out as the thrusting had her teetering toward an orgasm.

"Are you going to come?" he asked.

"Yes," she gasped and readied herself.

"No," he whispered and the dildo didn't come back in.

No? Teyla moaned, blinking in surprise. She stared at herself in the mirror and her mouth hung open in an un-attained gasp of frustration.

He moved her to the bed.

"Climb in," he ordered sharply, his voice hoarse with arousal.

She climbed in, holding up the covers for him to join her. Once beside her, he quickly swept her into his arms.

"Get on top of me. Ride me," he whispered into her ear.

Ride him?

Oh my, this command was a pleasant change. Most of her clients went directly for the missionary position.

Getting on her hands and knees, she whipped away the covers and caught the intense way he gazed up at her. That sexy look made her tummy hollow out in such a nice way.

Squatting over him, she lowered herself and angled her pussy over his engorged erection until she felt the smooth cockhead nudge against her vaginal opening.

He grinned up at her again. That damned smile of his flipped her out, distracting her from the job with all these butterfly sensations running through her body. Like wasn't she supposed to be pleasuring him? Instead, he was making her feel so wicked and wantonly hot, it was sinful.

His gaze raked her breasts as she maneuvered over his torso. He reached up, his hands melting like liquid fire over her waist as he guided her into the proper position over his engorged cock. She descended, her pussy enveloping his large girth. They both inhaled together as she crouched lower, his cock impaling her, the pressure unbelievable due to the plug in her ass.

"That's the way, babe," he whispered and hissed as he lifted her and brought her down onto his shaft again. Harder this time, making the breath suck right out of her lungs. Gosh, this felt so good.

She forced herself to keep her eyes open and study his reaction. His brown eyes were glazed with arousal and his smiling mouth twitched as he lifted her and brought her down on him again and again. As pleasure sparkled through her, she surveyed the dark, sexy stubble on his face, the thick column of his neck, his heavily muscled chest, and arms. And his scent. Oh wow, she really did like his scent. So alive and potent, it had her inhaling it deeply into her lungs and she felt her skin get nice and warm and her heart felt happy.

She noticed his smile had faded away and he was *really* looking at her too and *really* liking what he saw. Oh man, she was reading way too much into this again. Bad girl. Then the tips of his mouth twitched again as if he wanted to smile but he was holding himself back. That small movement ripped her out of her daydream state. Yep, better get back to reality or the guy was going to think she was some sort of nitwit.

As he brought her down again, his erection plunged deeper inside of her. She gyrated against his pelvis and he groaned. Her body tightened as carnal sensations grabbed and took hold. She could feel him tensing, knew he was going to come right along with her.

Mindless pleasure zapped out of nowhere, slamming into her. She bucked and gyrated as the pleasure raced through her like bolts of lightning. Oh, if this wasn't heaven, then she didn't know what it was.

He moaned raggedly and the erotic sound just about drove her crazy. She rode him as hard as she could, gyrating her hips against him, while he held tight to her breasts. Soon they were both sailing into the abyss of scorching passion and Teyla knew she'd never experienced anything so beautiful in her life.

Chapter Six

Logan found himself smiling as he listened to Teyla's soft breathing against his ear. They'd fallen asleep last night after that wild orgasm. Her on top of him, him still impaled inside of her. Just feeling her warm pussy clenched around his cock as she slept had him hardening quickly.

Man, he'd never been so damned horny with a woman before.

Usually, after a couple of fast fucks, he'd lose interest in the chick, but not with this one. He resisted the urge to reach up and stroke her hair. Resisted the urge to roll her over and start taking her again. Right now, he just wanted to enjoy how sweet it felt having her curves pressed up against him.

Yeah, real sweet. He could get used to this. Real used.

"A penny for your thoughts," a familiar male voice suddenly whispered from somewhere nearby and to his right.

Hell! If he hadn't immediately recognized the voice of one his partners' Spencer Greer, he'd be very caught right now, wouldn't he?

Shit! How come he hadn't heard anything? Man, he was really living on the edge with this woman, wasn't he?

"You can open your eyes, we know you're awake," his other partner, Cassidy Cane, murmured softly, obviously not wanting to wake up Teyla.

Logan opened his eyes and found the two men grinning down at him, very amused at having found him in this compromising position.

"She certainly does look good on you," Cassidy chuckled.

"And he means that quite literally," Spencer whispered.

"Great sense of humor, boys. Now get lost, I want some privacy."

"Privacy? Since when? You've never been bashful about being naked in front of us before."

There hadn't been quite this kind of woman before, he thought to himself.

He detected a shift in her breathing, realized she was slowing coming out of sleep mode. The last thing he wanted was for her to meet the guys while they were leering down at her.

"Get lost, gentleman, the lady is waking up and I don't want your ugly mugs to scare her off. You'll meet her in a bit."

"Your wish is our command, oh master," Cane's grin widened and he did a low sweeping bow, before he got nudged by Spencer, who urged him out of the bedroom.

Just in time too, because Teyla's pretty brown eyes fluttered open. She smiled at him and damned if his heart didn't do one hell of a neat flip.

Oh man, he was falling way too hard for this chick. He needed to freeze his heart. Keep this emotionless. It was after all, just a business transaction between them.

"I think I heard someone," she whispered, her entire body tensing.

"Yeah, well that would be the boys," he admitted.

She blinked sleepily, as if trying to figure out what he was saying and then recognition snapped through her face. Her smile wobbled and she swallowed. He wasn't sure if she was afraid or if she was nervous or excited, or maybe all three? Maybe he should ask her if she'd changed her mind?

"When did they come?" she asked and as she made a move to get off him, she inhaled softly, realizing he was still buried inside her. He could feel her vaginal muscles clench around his shaft a whole lot tighter.

Man, but she was sweet.

The guys would appreciate her. Just as much as he did. And he wanted to watch her get taken by them. It was a fetish of his. To share.

Man, he wanted to make love to her again. Now. But he'd wait. They had all day.

He forced the warmth out of his heart. Forced the emotions from him as well. Had she been his woman, he would have broken her in slowly. Just as he'd done his wife. But hell, those days were gone.

"Get dressed," he ordered.

She winced at the coldness in his voice and guilt slammed into him like a sledgehammer. He swore softly beneath his breath as she wiggled off him, her warm vagina reluctantly letting go of his stiff cock.

"I'll put the coffee on. Take your time. Make yourself pretty for them. They've been without a woman for a long time."

She nodded and as she stood, she grabbed a blanket off the bed and wrapped herself in it as if she were enveloping herself in a yellow cocoon, protecting herself from him.

Damn it! He was an asshole for acting so cold toward her.

He got out of bed, found his jeans, and climbed into them. He tried to ignore how cute she looked with that waterfall of messy silky brown hair tumbling all around her face while she watched him dress. Tried to resist this overwhelming urge to take her into his arms and give her a mind-blowing kiss. He took a step toward her, but laughter from the other two men from the kitchen area stopped him dead in his tracks.

Yeah, he needed to cool down. To get out there and away from her, or he'd end up in here the rest of the day. He needed to get updates from the boys regarding the posse and if they'd heard from the rest of the gang.

Grabbing his shirt, he headed for the bedroom door. When he reached it, he hesitated. He didn't want to leave without at least apologizing for his gruff order a moment earlier.

He turned around. His damned heart felt all warm and fuzzy as he saw that she was still watching him. Her cheeks were flushed; maybe she was embarrassed at the guys being here already? Or maybe she was just plain aroused at the prospect of three men taking her?

Well, whatever the case, she sure did look pretty with her hair all messy like that. No, more than pretty. She looked so damned sultry he wanted to kiss her yet again. Kiss away that pretty pout marring those luscious pink lips.

"I had a real good time last night. I just wanted to thank you for that," he blurted.

Her eyes widened slightly but she didn't say anything. Didn't smile.

Hell, what did he expect, anyways? It wasn't like they were lovers or something. Silently he kicked himself in his ass for having feelings of guilt, opened the door and stepped out of the room.

When Cassidy and Spencer saw him enter the kitchen, they must have noticed his confused state, because they suddenly stopped chuckling and eyed him with concern.

"What?" Spencer asked as he sat on the chair Teyla had used last night while they'd eaten the potatoes, bacon, and peaches.

Spencer had taken Logan's chair, his hand clutched around the empty peach can. If the guy had been trying to suck the last drops of syrup from the can he was out of luck. Logan had made sure he'd given Teyla most of the peach juice last night when he'd portioned out the peaches.

"What about the posse? Any sight of them?" Logan asked, ignoring Spencer's question.

They'd obviously gotten chilled during their ride over here because they'd stoked the stove with firewood and it was roaring and pumping out heat like a blast furnace. Despite that though, Logan couldn't shake off the coldness enveloping him regarding Teyla.

He should have kissed her. Reassured her that if she didn't want to go through with this ménage, she didn't have to. But, man, he wanted to share her. Wanted to watch the pleasure slash across her face when they took her.

Okay, so later he would ask if she'd changed her mind. Right now, they needed to get down to business.

"No sight of anyone and we did hear back from the rest of the gang through that lady doctor. She's quite a piece. Just as pretty as this woman you snagged for us," Spencer replied as he lifted the empty can above his mouth and awaited a sweet drop.

Logan grinned at the sight and at the compliment for Teyla. Damned right she was a pretty woman. No, a beautiful woman.

"You've got a tiger on your hands with that one," Cassidy chuckled from his perch. "A couple of men back in town spoke really highly of her. But they said she hadn't been getting much business, because she's refusing to put out for the banker, who owns the mortgage on her place. The banker is warning all her johns to stay away or else he will foreclose on their places. As luck would have it for her, the banker, also happens to be the self-appointed law in the nearest town to this place. He lived through the Catastrophe and kept his bank going and is insisting she keep making monthly payments on her farm or he'll foreclose on her."

Bastard. He hadn't known that fact about Teyla. Was that why she'd been so willing and hot in bed? To give him a good time on purpose? To get him hooked on her so he'd keep coming back?

Logan shook those stupid thoughts away. No, instincts told him she wasn't like that, but he certainly did feel a nasty burst of anger at the banker. He tamped down on his anger.

Emotions, my man. He couldn't get emotionally involved with a woman. He didn't want to get emotionally involved with any woman again. Losing his wife and kids had hurt too much.

Heck, wasn't that why he was in the situation he was in now? Because the grief over losing his wife and kids had made him want to do something to help out other people who'd found themselves in the similar situation, he'd found himself in after the Catastrophe?

Stealing from homes and being desperate enough to do just about anything to make sure his daughters were fed? He'd thought he was doing right by stealing from rich guys and giving to the poor. Now, after meeting Teyla, he wasn't so sure he wanted to do this anymore. He wanted to stay here and settle down with her.

He forced those thoughts away. He wouldn't go down the love road again. He just couldn't.

"So how is she in bed?" Cassidy asked as he suddenly bolted out of his chair and headed to the stove where he grabbed the steaming pot of coffee.

Both men's eager and expectant gazes snapped to Logan's face. They hadn't had a woman in weeks. Desperate to lose themselves in female company, the three of them shared the fetish for sharing and had agreed to celebrate their latest victory with one woman.

"She won't disappoint," Logan said truthfully.

"So? She's agreed to the terms then?" Spencer replied not bothering to conceal his excitement.

"She's agreed." Or at least he hoped she hadn't changed her mind.

Both men whooped and Logan shook his head at their excitement. He couldn't blame them. It wasn't easy to find a woman willing to accommodate three men at once and they sure weren't going to disappoint Teyla.

"The barn is ready for the horses. You'll find everything you need for them in there," Logan said, hoping they would take the hint and get out.

"Horses are already bedded down," Cassidy replied.

"Okay, then there's a hand pump with some soap. Here are a couple of towels." Logan opened up a nearby closet which he'd already checked last night when he'd first come into her farmhouse. He remembered seeing towels in there. He handed each of them one.

"I'll get her ready," he said. Truth be told he wanted some more alone time with her. To make sure she really was ready. Or maybe it was he who wasn't ready to share her?

Teyla scolded herself for being bothered by Logan's sharp voice when he'd told her earlier to get dressed. He was paying her to do a job, pure and simple. And now with his two friends showing up, she was required to participate in the next phase of their agreement. She just wished she could have had a little more alone time with him.

Last night he'd opened to her about his past. About his wife, his daughters. He'd been gentle, yet rough in their lovemaking. She'd even fallen asleep on top of him, with him buried inside of her. She'd never done *that* with a client before. She'd never done that with Max before either.

It had felt good waking up that way with his arms around her, his cock buried inside her and his butt plug inside her.

Teyla blew out a tense breath. He'd said he'd enjoyed last night. Said it with such a softness in his voice, such a tender sparkle in his eyes, she hadn't been able to respond with all the fluttery sensations zipping through her.

She wondered how his friends looked like. She'd been asleep and had heard Logan talking to them, but she'd felt so safe and comfortable in his arms it had been a struggle to wake up. And when she had, those men had already retreated to the next room.

Washing carefully between her legs, she listened to the kitchen door open and close. Listened to two sets of boots stomp over the boards of the veranda and down the stairs and found herself tensing when she heard the floorboards in the next room creak beneath the weight of someone.

Logan? Or had he decided to let one of his friends join her first?

Teyla licked her suddenly dry lips and quickly finished her washing, tossing the washcloth into the basin. As the door creaked open, she grabbed her robe, holding it up in front of her. She held her breath, and let out a slow sigh of relief when Logan walked in.

When he saw her standing there, her robe clutched in front of her, she could tell in the heated way he looked at her, he wanted to take her again. And she wanted him to too. Wanted him to sweep her into his arms and make her feel safe, secure, and loved.

Oh boy, she really was turning into some delusional needy woman, wasn't she?

"They brought you a letter from that lady doctor friend of yours," Logan said and strolled toward her.

He held the letter in question out to her and she took it. She didn't really have to open it; she could already tell it was from Dr. Liz from the familiar perfume that sifted comfortingly off the letter, but she thought it in her best interest to read it, just in case there was something she should know about the men's health.

Holding her robe with one hand, she ripped the sealed envelope at the edge by her teeth and brought out the letter. Liz's feminine handwriting greeted her and Teyla hadn't even realized she was tense until she relaxed as she read the letter. Dr. Liz had given both the newcomers a clean bill of health. And then at the end of the letter, she'd once again added for Teyla to let her know if size counts.

Oh man. Three well hung men. This was going to be very interesting, indeed.

"I think we know each other well enough that you don't need to cover yourself," Logan said smoothly as he watched her fold the letter and settle it and the envelope onto the dresser on top of the other one that Dr. Liz had sent with Logan.

Tremors of anticipation snapped through her like live wires and Teyla dropped the robe to the floor, creaming warmly when his gaze zeroed onto her nude pussy.

He licked his lips and her breaths hitched. He seemed like a predatory animal. Full of intent. Danger. Sexual.

His potent scent, of the sex they'd had, poured off him in hot waves.

"Turn around," he whispered.

His voice sounded gruff and aroused as he placed his strong hands on her bare shoulders and led her toward the closest bedroom window.

Earlier, before she'd started cleaning herself up, she'd opened the curtains and now as she stood in front of the window she could see out into the yard. Could see his two friends stripping off their shirts in front of her red water pump.

Fissures of excitement rippled through her as she watched huge muscles bulge in their arms. One of the men began to pump and water cascaded out. The other yelped as he splashed the freezing water over a well-muscled wide chest.

The taller of the two was dark brown haired and tanned. His hair was short and brushed to one side. The other man, looked thinner, his hair was also dark brown and cascaded past his shoulders. He looked well-muscled. They both wore tight jeans that rode low on their hips and cowboy style boots.

"The one with longer hair is Cassidy and the other one is Spencer," Logan said as he massaged her shoulders. She expected him to move her away from the window for all the two men had to do was look and she'd be seen standing her naked.

But he didn't.

He just kept massaging her shoulders, digging his fingers into her tense muscles.

"Let's give them a glimpse of what they'll be getting, shall we?"

She inhaled as his hands moved off her shoulders and came around to cup her breasts. At the same time, he pressed his body against her, bringing her closer to the window. He pushed against her until her breasts were squished against the cold windowpane and then he dipped his head and kissed her left shoulder with a gentle butterfly kiss that sent shimmers of pleasure down her spine. A guttural whimper found itself passing her lips. It was a sexy sound she really liked.

"I thought I would come in and see if you were okay with the ménage. I can see that you are."

She nodded jerkily. Okay, so maybe he was sure, but was she really?

"I wanted you to meet them first, but then I figured it might be better this way."

This way? What exactly did he mean?

"At least then you wouldn't have to feel self-conscious before...," he let the words trail off. She still wasn't sure what he meant and then suddenly she noticed the two men at the pump had stopped washing themselves and were looking directly at the window where she stood.

"They're very observant men," Logan chuckled. "Nothing gets by them."

She thought she would feel embarrassed at having been found like this, oddly enough, she wasn't.

"Invite them in, when you're ready," Logan purred into her ear, his wet tongue lashing her earlobe with sultry licks.

Invite them in when you're ready.

Was she ready? Would she ever be? Was he giving her a way out? This was the first time in her life she'd ever been asked to do this sort of thing. Sure, she'd fantasized. But fantasy was so different in reality.

This felt surreal. And fantastic.

She had to be crazy. But she felt so feminine and sexy to have two men looking at her and another one touching her. Wonderfully insane and it felt so liberating to embrace her sexuality in this way.

Through heavy lidded eyes, she watched the two of them as they stared at her, and then suddenly as if with a mind of its own she lifted her right hand and crooked a finger at them, inviting them to come inside. Their mouths dropped open as if they couldn't believe what she was doing.

"That's it, Teyla. Invite them in," Logan breathed against her hair as he lashed her earlobe with more sultry kisses that sent arrays of excitement shimmering through her. With her heart pounding loudly in her ears, her body sandwiched between the window and Logan, she watched the two men finish washing and then hurry toward the farmhouse. Toward her.

Panic zipped through her.

Oh God! What had she gotten into? Three men and her?

She swallowed as Logan gyrated his large erection against her butt plug. It pushed deeper into her, the invasion sensual and erotic. She stiffened against him as she heard the front door creak open, followed by the stomping sounds of their boots.

"They'll be gentle with you, at first, so just relax," he whispered.

He moved away from her, allowing her to budge from the window. His hands dropped from her breasts and she turned around to face him.

"I want you to climb onto the bed. On your elbows and knees, head down on the bed, face sideways into a pillow. Your ass in the air. Your breasts hanging and your nipples just grazing the blankets. I'll bring them in once you're in the position."

Teyla creamed at his words, at the agonized look of arousal splashing across his face.

She nodded jerkily and climbed onto the bed while he watched. Her face grew warm as she tried to remember his instructions and imagined how she would look to them. Her face buried against the pillow, her elbows bracing herself on the bed, breasts dangling, her ass plugged and stuck up in the air like an offering.

Sweet mercy! They would be doing more than just gazing!

She blew out a tense breath and she stayed in that position listening to their low murmurs from the kitchen. She tensed at the knock at the door and Logan's abrupt answer instructing them to enter.

She swore her breath stalled in her lungs when she heard their soft whistles.

"Fantastic," one of them said softly. Instantly she liked his voice. Soft and low. Comforting.

"She's more than fantastic, Spencer. She's gorgeous," the other one, Cassidy, replied.

"Close your eyes, Teyla. Remain in that position while the guys touch you."

Oh my God.

Her pussy creamed harder and her tummy dipped with an incredible feeling. She tensed as she sensed the men coming closer. Could feel them as the air around her became thick with sexual tension.

Strange that no fear held her. No embarrassment. Just pure excitement. And disbelief. It seemed as if she were meant to be here. An object of their lust. A woman to be pleasured and to be someone else's pleasure.

Such a simple thought, yet such a complicated feat against the morals that had been drilled into her since an early age. If things hadn't been so desperate, would she have accepted these three strangers?

Truthfully, she'd been lonely out here. No one to talk to except the occasional client who dare defy the banker-sheriff.

Her occasional client would be greedy. They always were. Not taking the time to pleasure her. He'd just slap the money down and she'd end up sobbing after he was gone. Weeping at what she'd become. But with Logan, it had been different. He'd taken her pleasure into consideration, but would she end up crying into the pillow after he left?

Truly? She hoped not, but probably. He'd brought her a renewed feeling of worth and with these three men in the room, their gazes on her nude body, their hoarse breaths snapping through the air like whips, she wanted what was to come next. Wanted this bad.

She yelped in surprise when a warm hand cupped her right breast.

"Easy, I've got you, babe." Logan's tender voice whispered like silk over her alert nerve endings, calming her sudden flare of uneasiness.

Wow, for a few seconds there, she'd been so carefree. Now she seemed to have sunk back into doubt. From her other side, someone cupped her other breast. This hand was calloused, not as hot. But she could smell the soap he'd used out by the pump.

"I've got you too." She recognized the voice of the one called Spencer.

She nodded clumsily and he squeezed her nipple between his thumb and a finger. Then both of her nipples were being plucked and kneaded. To her surprise, a wondrous pulsing beat sprang between her thighs.

A pair of hot hands lightly covered her ass cheeks and the third man's deep voice curled like melted chocolate over her senses.

"I've got your backside, sweetie." Cassidy.

A sharp slap to her ass had her yelping at the pain, but hot hands soothed her fiery flesh with gentle caresses. A few more heavy slaps and her ass was literally burning and truth be told, she was enjoying it.

Peeking sideways, she caught a glimpse of herself in the mirror and her mouth dropped open in wonder at the sight. Her cheeks were flushed red on both her ass and her face.

"You like getting spanked, don't you, honey?" Cassidy asked. He didn't wait for an answer as a finger swept between her pussy lips and grazed her vaginal opening.

"Oh yeah, she does. She's soaking, Logan. You didn't tell us she liked getting spanked."

"You didn't ask," Logan said in a thick, heavy voice that sent a wild buzz through Teyla. Obviously, he'd gotten turned on watching her getting spanked.

"Besides," he continued, "she wasn't being bad with me, so I never really had a reason to give her a really good hard spanking. But I must admit her ass does blush nicely."

"I'd say she's being bad now, Logan, my man. She's got two other men in her bed, besides you. Don't you think that's reason enough for you to take over the spanking department?"

"Yeah, I like watching a woman get her ass spanked and I like spanking her even more," Logan murmured.

Oh God. Teyla tensed as she creamed and listened to the rough breathing of her three men. She could hear them moving behind her. Then she gasped as a sharp sting snapped against her cheeks. She didn't have to see who slapped her. She knew it was Logan in the restrained way his palm touched her flesh. He didn't want to hurt her. Wasn't as rough as the other one, but the effect was just as potent, if not more.

Logan slapped her ass a few more times until she burned and yearned for him to stop. When he finally did, he swept his hand between her legs and cupped her pussy with his palm. Pressing firmly, he gyrated his palm along her sensitized clit.

She bit back a moan as wicked tension sifted through her. Just as she started falling into the abyss of pleasure, he stopped grinding and chuckled knowingly, removing his hand.

"I'm pleased you enjoyed your punishment, Teyla."

She held her breath as the other man began caressing her burning ass again with tender strokes. Logan returned to her side and she expected him to begin stroking her breasts again. To her disappointment he didn't. Instead, he produced a black blindfold and placed it over her eyes. She smelled his scent on it. Musk and sweat and pine. Very nice.

The darkness was alluring, yet also frightening. She'd been paid handsomely for giving three men access to her body and once again uneasiness lashed her.

What if they hurt her? Humiliated her? Told her neighbors what they'd done with her? Another shot of heat blazed across her face at that last thought, and she swallowed as someone gently tugged the butt plug from her hole.

Involuntarily her anus spasmed and clenched, aching to be filled again. She ached to be filled by all three of them.

Oh, sweet mercy! She'd never experienced such lust, such carnal need. She couldn't stop herself from moaning her frustration, her need.

"Take it easy baby," Logan's hoarse whisper sped over her senses like ribbons of velvet.

She whimpered in answer, suddenly unable to speak. Unable to do anything but feel their caressing hands upon her flesh.

"Now let's take this off the bed so we can continue arousing you."

Shivers skittered through her at what he said. She nodded curtly as she was led off the bed. Her legs were wobbly, and if the two men hadn't been holding her, she swore she would have dropped to the floor.

All three of them caressed her, their strong hands melting over her shoulders, her waist, and legs.

Logan stood in front of her. She could smell him. His dominating scent made her tremble with a sexual need so fierce it was animalistic. Untamed. Wickedly delightful.

He began kissing her, his lips melting like liquid fire against hers. Meanwhile their hands continued to touch, to tease, to seduce every part of her. It wasn't long before exhilaration raged through her and she gripped Logan's waist tightly, keening at this pleasure.

To her surprise, Logan chuckled against her mouth, breaking the deep kisses.

"Was wondering when you'd start loosening up, babe. It'll feel much better when you do." His voice sparkled. He sounded happy and it made her heart smile.

He leaned in and kissed the erotic area behind her earlobe splashing wonderful sensations through her. He sucked her earlobe into his mouth and did such erotic things to her ear with his tongue, he had her trembling and barely catching her breath. Yes, he certainly did have a way with that tongue of his and he chased away her fears all too quickly.

One of the other two men, she wasn't sure which, but knew it wasn't Logan because of his restrained roughness, massaged her breasts. He certainly knew how to handle them, for he expertly stroked her nipples, pinching and brushing his fingers firmly over them until she felt as if she were just two breasts. Weird to think that way, but she was.

Behind her, the third man slipped his hands around her waist and pressed himself against her backside, letting her feel the impression of his very hot and swollen cock against her left ass cheek.

Oh my. He felt big. Just like Logan.

"Are you okay?" Logan whispered as he leaned in and kissed her chin.

She nodded.

"It's been quite some time, since..."

She inhaled a trembling breath, wanting to tell him it had been a while since she'd done anal, but the words just didn't come out of her mouth.

Mainly because she wasn't sure if her confession might make them stop and she didn't want them to stop. Now that she'd come this far, she was too keened and curious to find out what would happen next.

"You're doing fine. Now just try to relax so we can entertain you, sweets."

Have mercy. She was being paid to have sex with them, and they were entertaining *her*? What kind of men were they to put her pleasure before their own?

She forced herself to inhale, to loosen up. But how could any sane woman relax with three men touching her? At that thought she almost burst out laughing as a tinge of hysteria shot though her. What would her female friends say if they found out? They'd think she was crazy or maybe they'd be envious?

Fingers increased pressure on her nipples and she refocused back to the men.

Her men.

Sweet Lord.

More pressure from that large cock snapped against her left ass cheek. It made her dig her fingers into Logan's waist. Made her wonder how it would feel like to have these two newcomers having sex with her with Logan in the room, watching.

"You like this, don't you, Teyla? Three men about to make love to you." Logan breathed. "I can see it in the way you're smiling. The way your nipples have become engorged. The way you're creaming."

She whimpered in agreement.

Maybe other woman didn't appreciate a ménage, but she did.

Oh yes, she did!

Chapter Seven

"Okay, guys. Let's take this into the living room, now. I saw an armchair that will work for what we want to do to her." It was Logan speaking, his voice thick with arousal.

The living room? She'd never had sex before in her living room. She always kept her guests in here. She didn't dare mount a protest. She was too curious to see what they were up to.

Because she wore a blindfold, they led her. She knew when they entered the kitchen as it was warmer out here and then she knew when they'd entered the living room because it was cooler. She shivered as the cool air breathed against her naked skin and hoped one of the men would make a fire in the fireplace.

That's what she loved about her century old farmhouse. A fireplace in every room.

Beneath her bare feet, the cold, old floorboards creaked, and it didn't take but a moment when she heard the squeak of the armchair as someone sat on it.

Logan? It must be him because the two men holding her upper arms didn't smell like him.

"I hope someone brought the lube? And some condoms?" Logan asked.

Yes, it was him sitting on the chair. Happiness bubbled inside her as she guessed what he was up to.

"Here," Cassidy said.

She heard the sound of something slapping against flesh and then another and she pictured Logan catching the tube of lube and a box of condoms. Imagined him, sitting there on her couch, naked, his big cock engorged as he waited for her to join him there.

She shivered again as she heard foil being ripped open. A moan as he rolled on the condom and then the squirt of lube and slurps of it being lathered on his cock.

This time she didn't tremble from the cold but from the anticipation slicing through her. She whimpered. Both her butt and vaginal muscles clenched with a need for action. To be filled.

"Easy, babe. We're hurrying as fast as we can," Spencer whispered in her ear. His voice was drenched with lust and amusement.

Cassidy let go of her and Spencer was maneuvering her around. She felt slightly off balance with the blindfold but then someone grabbed both her hands and intertwined his fingers with hers. She relaxed, instinctively knowing Logan's touch from last night when they'd walked and held hands. He was behind her. Waiting for her.

Spencer continued to hold her upper arms and she listened to Cassidy as he lit a match. She heard it flare to life and smelled the sulfur. A moment later, a fire began to crackle in the fireplace.

"It's a good idea you have keeping the wood and kindling in the hearth ready to go. Cuts down on time," Cassidy said from her right where the fireplace was located. She didn't say anything to his compliment. She had better things to think about. Like was her ass going to be able to handle Logan's big size?

She trembled again at that thought.

"Cold, baby? No worries, we'll warm you up, right, Logan?" Spencer said.

"She'll be so hot, she'll be burning with the three of us taking her," came Logan's confident reply.

His deep voice melted over her like fireworks and she could feel her every sense tuning into him. Into them. Her every nerve firing.

Spencer continued to hold her upper arm as Logan pulled her backward by the hands.

"Okay, now squat down, baby. Sit on my lap. I'm so hard for you."

She swallowed, warmed at his comment. Oh yeah, he was right. She would be burning soon.

She did as he asked and as she slowly sat, his hot solid as a pole cock nudged against the tight hole of her ass.

Okay. She knew what they were up to now and excitement flared to a whole new level. Holding his fingers tightly for balance and reassurance, she squatted lower, allowing his erection to press past her tight sphincter muscles. She gasped at the bite of pleasure pain as he sunk deep into her, the pressure unbelievable. Sitting upon his lap, she was now fully impaled and gasping at the incredible pleasure pain and pressure buried inside her ass.

Logan moaned and let go of her hands.

"Come, grab the armchair and lay back on me," he instructed.

She found the armchair rests and did as he asked, leaning back, and inhaled harshly as his cock sunk deeper and his warm broad chest nestled warmly against her back.

"Widen her legs and angle them up on each side of my knees. Then I can hold her open for one of you."

Oh, sweet mercy. That suggestion had her creaming really hard.

Hands did as he asked and they spread her, placing her legs over his. She was amazed she was this flexible, but figured it was due to that demanding work in the greenhouse and all the natural eating she'd been doing since the Catastrophe. Oh Teyla, stop thinking about that, just concentrate on what they are doing!

Logan tilted them both back as he leaned against the armchair and she could only imagine how she must look to the two men with her legs wide open, her ass impaled on Logan, her pussy wet and open, waiting to be penetrated by one of them.

"Tie her hands to the chair," Logan ordered.

She tensed remembering their conversation about bondage.

"Don't worry, your legs will be free, not that you'll want to kick anyone away." She heard the humor in his otherwise lust-thickened voice.

She bit her bottom lip with a sudden bout of worry as her wrists were lashed to the chair.

"That's it, baby. Let them tie you down."

She couldn't believe how hard she creamed at his soothing tone of approval. When she tried to move her wrists, she realized that if she pulled really hard, she'd be free. She decided not to. If Logan got turned on by watching her arms restrained, then that was all that mattered. She was here to please. All of them.

Calloused hands nestled upon her thighs and without warning two sets of mouths nestled over her breasts, warm moist lips taking her nipples hostage making her moan at the delightful sensations zipping through her body.

Wow! She hadn't expected this!

A hand cupped her pussy, hot, heavy, and once again she tensed, her senses raw and alert, wondering what was going to happen next. The pressure of a palm increased and whoever touched her there began a slow erotic grinding motion against her clit. The touches had her breathing faster and creaming harder.

She leaned her head back and turned her face to find Logan's mouth. He kissed her, his lips dominant and confident.

Once again, the men touched her skin, fingers exploring her every crevice as they massaged and caressed.

Shock waves of wonder snapped through her like live wires. She'd never been touched by so many hands before. So many men.

Incredible sensations lashed her and she was suddenly just a body enjoying pleasure. A blank mind. Nothing else existed but their touches, their mouths, their teeth biting her nipples, tongues lashing and licking her breasts. A firm hot palm grinding against her pussy.

She felt someone's hands in her hair. Logan's kiss intensified. The palm left her pussy. The mouths abandoned her breasts.

She heard the rip of foil. Condom.

Thankfully, *they* were thinking.

Anticipation raced through her as a sheathed cock nudged against her vagina. The hands in her hair tightened some more. Logan's kiss intensified. His tongue sliding into her mouth, dueling with hers. It seemed as if Logan wanted to make sure that she knew he was here for her. That despite someone else about to have sex with her, he was the main guy. Or maybe it was just wishful thinking on her part, but that's what she was feeling.

The cock coming into her vagina was big. Understandably a tight fit, due to her ass being impaled on Logan.

She whimpered as the pressure built. Felt hard, powerful hands nestling beside her bound wrists on the armchair. She pictured the man bracing himself with his arms so he wouldn't put his entire weight on her and Logan. As the cock in her pussy withdrew, fire raced through her.

She whimpered into Logan's mouth, curled her hands into fists, and instinctively arched her hips, accepting more of this man's solid girth. She wondered which one he was. Cassidy? Or Spencer.

From somewhere nearby, she heard the other one toss more wood on the fire. It was getting really warm in here now with Logan kissing her and the other one taking her pussy. He started with slow thrusts, and then quickly moved faster with more confident plunges.

Logan stopped his kiss and she cried out in protest. But his hands were holding her tight, angling her head a little and to her shock she felt hard smooth flesh press against her lips.

A cock? How in the world?

"Open your mouth for Spencer, sweetness. He's up on the table beside the sofa all nice and ready for you," Logan groaned.

She did as he asked and her lips stretched to accommodate his hugeness.

"Nod when I hit the back of your throat, baby," Spencer said in a low guttural voice. When his thick, smooth cockhead touched the back of her throat, she nodded. She realized he would be wrapping his hand around his cock at one point, ensuring he didn't go too far in. That thought totally relaxed her. They were thinking about not hurting her and finally she allowed trust to melt through her.

She would enjoy this and not doubt them. She would accept what they did to her. This was good.

And as if her body sensed her mind accepting, she exploded into a fantastic orgasm. Her mind shattered, and she moaned around Spencer's plunging cock as he pistoned into her mouth and Cassidy pistoned into her pussy.

Beneath her, Logan moaned as she bucked and gyrated, eagerly accepting Spencer's and Cassidy's thrusts.

"That's it, baby. Go with it," he said between gritted teeth.

He said other words in a soothing tone, but she was oblivious. She was arching her hips, tightening her legs as she opened herself up more for Spencer.

"Oh, yeah," she heard Spencer growl. His thrusts became faster, more powerful.

Beneath her, Logan's cock pulsed and tightened and she realized Spencer's pounding onto her pussy was causing some sort of friction for Logan too.

Cassidy drove his condom covered cock into her mouth, pistoning into her in the same fast and confident rhythm as Spencer. Having three cocks inside her encouraged her to go wild. She thrashed beneath them and simply gave into her instincts. Became lost in her senses as a female, a woman being made love to by three strangers.

Spencer kept up his hard bucks, powering into her. His strong hips pounded against her hips as he stroked his long thick cock in and out of her. She heard the slurp of her juices as he pistoned. Heard all three men moaning and groaning as they took her.

She grew heady and hot. Her lips felt swollen from Cassidy's swift plunges. Her tongue grew tired as she continued licking underneath Cassidy's cock and suctioned her mouth tighter and tighter every time, he plunged into her.

Then he gave out a strangled groan and she felt his cock swell and tighten against her tongue. Felt the condom begin to bulge as it filled with his heated release and then he withdrew.

Suddenly the blindfold was ripped away and she opened her eyes to see Cassidy's naked form move away from the table beside the armchair. She turned her head and watched Spencer as he continued to thrust into her. His eyes were closed and pure raw pleasure wrenched his face. Her tummy hollowed out at the sight that a man could look so erotic while he had sex with her.

"Hey babe, kiss me. I miss you," Logan moaned and she angled her head so their lips melted together again.

Spencer's thrusts increased and she could feel his lower half tightening against her widespread legs. Logan's lips pressed harder into her and his body also tightened as Spencer's pistoning became more powerful. Within seconds both men's cocks seemed to thicken inside her and they cried out in their heated release.

She was drained, her body covered in a sheen of perspiration. Aside from heavy breathing, the crackling of the fire and someone getting dressed, the silence in the room was overpowering.

"Make a bath for her," she heard Logan say as Spencer withdrew from her. Someone untied her wrists, but she was too tired to move her hands or keep her eyes open. She must have drifted off because she didn't remember being removed from Logan because when she came to, she was being carried in a pair of strong arms. Instinctively she knew he wasn't Logan. He didn't smell like him, but in the tender way he held her, she knew she was safe and snuggled up against a strong hot naked chest.

"Where are you taking me?" she mumbled sleepily, not wanting to open her eyes. Not wanting to know who was carrying her. Oh heck, who was she kidding? She was feeling all embarrassed now that she'd had sex with three strangers.

"Getting you a nice hot bath," the gruff male voice she recognized as Spencer said. Yes, the beauty of having a solar heated water tank. Always hot water for a bath after her clients visited. In this case, three clients. Wowsa!

Balmy steam curled around her as they entered the bathroom. She smiled, feeling giddy and sexually satisfied and oh so pleasantly sore yet unpleasantly sticky between her thighs and ass as he gently lowered her into the water. To her surprise, little bubbles snapped and burst and caressed her sensitive ass and pussy.

Lavender scent of her favorite bubble bath, one that she hadn't used since the Catastrophe, wafted up from the steam and for a split second Teyla thought of the man placing her in the tub as being Logan. Logan as her husband and they were about to enjoy a bath together.

That lovely thought disintegrated as the warm water whispered over her flesh and her eyes snapped open to gaze straight into Spencer's dark green eyes.

Wow, he certainly did have the nicest color of eyes, she thought as he tenderly set her into the tub. And damned if her face didn't feel too hot as another shot of embarrassment whipped through her. This man, this complete stranger, and his friend, as well as Logan, had just had sex with her. And now he'd lowered her naked body into a tub of water and maybe even wanted more sex.

She was tired. Kind of, anyways, and suddenly she wished she could just sink her head into the froth of bubbles and not come up until he was gone.

"Okay, so what are you doing with my woman?" Logan's voice echoed from the doorway.

To her surprise, Teyla sighed in relief at having Logan nearby. Not that she did not like this guy. She just, didn't know him. It felt awkward and she wondered where the other one had gotten off to.

"Hey, I thought we were sharing," Spencer grinned down at her and winked. He looked so sexy and friendly when he did that and Teyla instinctively realized this guy would never harm her.

"She's too pretty to share. Now get out. I'm feeling like a bath myself."

"Looks like room enough for three in the tub," Spencer replied as he unfolded his tall body and stood.

My oh my, he was a tall one. Even taller than Logan, Teyla realized as she looked up at the giant of a man.

Logan ignored his comment, his gaze snapping to hers and holding it.

"You stay there. I'll be back in a minute."

Her heart thumped with wicked anticipation as both men left the bathroom. Logan had called her pretty. Too pretty to share. A giddy warmth gushed through her and she chastised herself for thinking such silliness.

He was just being nice. That's all. And of course, wanting to have more sex?

She didn't have time to contemplate that last thought when the door burst open wider and Logan stepped back in. He carried a tray, she recognized as one she kept in her kitchen closet. She spied a wine bottle, two wine glasses and a small vase of wildflowers.

"Now where in the world did you find those?" She hadn't seen wildflowers since before the Catastrophe.

"Well, I could take the compliment myself and pretend I ordered them especially for you, but it was Cassidy who found them up in a sheltered field in the next valley on their way over here. He picked them for you. He just didn't get the chance to give it you, since I told him I wanted more alone time with you."

Logan wanted more alone time. How sweet. And she wanted some more with him too.

"I'll have to thank him for the flowers when I see him." After the bath. After another romp with Logan.

The flowers looked gorgeous. Goldenrods and some purple ones that looked like mini daisies. She didn't know the name of them, but she knew they were both fall flowers. And it was only June. Crazy weather.

"And this," he held up the bottle of red wine, which these days must cost a fortune, and grinned, "is to celebrate your first time at a ménage."

"A most wonderful time," she replied truthfully, although her cheeks must be getting so beet red, because they felt awfully toasty with him staring at her the way he was. Like a man who wanted to feast upon her again. Although she'd only known him now for almost twenty-four hours, she already recognized the look of desire and need in his eyes. The look of wanting sex from her. It made her shiver and warm and excited all wrapped up like a snuggly blanket.

She watched him pour the wine and accepted the glass, giggling.

"What's so funny? he asked, quirking an eyebrow in puzzlement.

"I haven't had wine since I can't even remember. It's way too expensive in town."

She could pay off the mortgage on her land selling this bottle alone. Where did he get such money? He had to be into something illegal to be able to afford wine. That thought was quickly forgotten as he dropped his pants revealing quite the solid erection.

Mercy! The man never went to sleep, did he?

"Wiggle your legs up baby. I'm joining you."

She moved her legs and he climbed into the claw foot tub, settling in front of her, his feet coming in on the insides of each leg. She gasped as his foot nudged up between her thighs, his toes nestling against her pussy.

"Foot sex. Ever tried it?" He asked as he reached for his drink.

Sex in the tub? Was he serious? Did he have a foot fetish?

"Um no, but it does sound intriguing."

She watched him sip his wine. Loved the way his full lips melted over the glass. Enjoyed the bobbing of his Adams apple, as he drank. When he drew the glass away wine sparkled like burgundy jewels on his mouth. And suddenly she wanted to kiss him. Bad.

But his foot moved against her pussy, a hot firm toe pressed between her labia and he tenderly massaged her clit. She sipped her wine, watching him studying her, trying hard not to moan as erotic sensations shimmered through her.

"So how did you enjoy being taken by three men?"

Wow. Nice question. Nice sensations shimmering through her pleasantly sore pussy too.

"Wasn't it obvious?" she teased.

"Very. But I want to hear it in your words. How did it feel being double penetrated and a cock coming into your mouth all at the same time?"

Oh dear. Here goes the bold talk again. She creamed against his toes and her cheeks went even hotter. She wished she could dive beneath the bubbles and disappear from his questioning and sexy stare.

"Does it turn you on, if I talk dirty?" she asked and noticed it was his turn to shift uncomfortably.

"Because I can talk really dirty. Having a big cock in my mouth plunging in and out made me want you inside my pussy. Hot and heavy. Fast and furious strokes and..."

"Jesus, woman. You keep talking like that and I'll have to call in the boys again."

Her heart was pounding at the huskiness in his voice. Her breasts felt heavy and with the erotic feel of water lapping against them and the bubbles caressing her nipples, she was feeling turned on.

Inadvertently, she nudged her toes against his big cock and she gasped at how hot and throbbing his swollen flesh felt against her. By the solid thickness and firmness, he certainly was ready to go another round. And truth be told so was she.

Moving her foot, she anchored it against his scrotum and kneaded gently. He groaned. Grinned.

"You are a vixen, aren't you?"

"Two can play at this game," she joked.

They touched each other that way, using their toes and feet to arouse each other while they leisurely sipped their wine. His breaths came faster. Hers, just as quick.

Wicked sensations swept through her. Her body tightened as she flew toward an orgasm. As she exploded, her body twisted and thrashed against the bubbles. Her wine goblet, suddenly forgotten on the bathtub rim, fell over and smashed against the bathroom floor with an ear shattering sound, joining the splash of water, her whimpers, and his guttural groans as he came right along with her.

The throes of the orgasm left her weary and the effects of the wine made her heady. She could feel herself relaxing in the afterglow of sex. The soft scent of bubbles and warm water wrapped around her like a cocoon. Made her feel safe. Safe and sleepy.

Chapter Eight

Logan watched her eyes drift closed. His heart warmed. Something it hadn't done in years.

Gorgeous woman, very easy to fall for her. Too easy. What would happen to her when they left?

She was strong. Could maybe hold out for another couple of years. But if something happened to her greenhouse and her food ran out? What would happen to her? What if the weather continued to get colder as scientists predicted? Her greenhouse wouldn't produce much. Plants and solar panels needed sunshine and warmth. He knew that much about planting even if he was brought up a city kid.

What *was* going to happen to her? He asked himself again, the nice momentary warmth disappearing from his heart.

What if he stayed?

He stiffened as he heard the soft footsteps in the bedroom.

Uneasiness zipped through him like a torpedo. Had the guys returned? Or was it someone else?

He'd left his gun out in his jacket on the hanger in the kitchen! The rest were in his saddlebag. Earlier today when the guys had arrived, he hadn't noticed the saddlebag around either. Had one of the boys moved it?

Dammit! He'd been so enthralled with Teyla, he'd forgotten to be alert. How could he have been so damn stupid?

Logan held his breath, quickly swept the wine bottle from the floor, and readied himself to smash it over the edge of the tub. He'd use the jagged edges as a weapon. A whole hell of a lot good it would be if the intruder had a gun, though.

A floorboard creaked.

He readied himself to stand, but realized if he did, the water dripping from his body into the tub would let the intruder know someone was in here. He'd have to wait until he saw someone stepping inside the bathroom.

As if sensing a problem, Teyla's eyes snapped open.

Quickly he lifted a finger to his mouth and motioned to her to be quiet. Her eyes darted to toward the slightly open doorway. Back to him again. She shook her head, lifted her hand out of the quickly dissolving bubbles, signaling him to stay put.

Before he could stop her. She rose out of the tub and took a few steps forward.

Any other time, watching her naked wet pink flesh caressed here and there with bubbles would have him reaching out grabbing her and pulling her right back into the bathtub on top of him. That erotic thought died when he heard someone breathing.

He knew enough about his partners breathing to know it wasn't either of them. A nasty feeling of sickness crawled through his belly thinking Cassidy and Spencer might have been taken out.

It wasn't like them to not give him a warning. Something bad must've happened to them. Something really bad.

Logan readied the bottle. He'd crack it now and rush the intruder. As if sensing what he was thinking, Teyla shook her head, once again motioning for him to remain in the tub.

She grabbed a robe hanging off the hook and put it on. Without another glance at him, she walked out of the bathroom. closing the door firmly behind her.

Fuck!

Teyla's knees literally shook as she closed the door behind her and came face-to-face with the law.

"Linus? I didn't hear you knock?" She tried to keep the anger out of her voice, but it was hard.

Linus McWilliams, the self-appointed sheriff around these parts was a constant thorn in her side. Not only was he the law, but he was also the banker who held the mortgage on her land. She'd never liked the creepy way he looked at her with the palest blue eyes. He wore his blond hair in a short military cut and had a large moustache that curled upwards at the sides.

He was a short, plump man with a red face who was always dropping in on her uninvited, pretending to check up on her. But what he really wanted was to have sex with her. She'd told him many times she didn't service married men. Under any conditions. He'd been pretty much the only man she knew whose wife had survived the Catastrophe. All other couples she'd known had lost their partners.

"I knocked, but you must not have heard," he replied, but she could read the lie quite clearly in his eyes.

Like hell he'd knocked. She'd been drifting leisurely in the after-sex glow, but she hadn't been asleep. She'd been enjoying the sounds of Logan's easy breathing. The way his cock had been swelling once again against her foot, but she hadn't heard anything aside from the creak on the floor of her bedroom to indicate someone had entered.

"I was bathing," she explained, casting him a smile she certainly didn't feel.

Inside, she felt cold toward him and couldn't wait for him to be gone.

"I had a customer. You just missed him," she explained.

His smile dropped at the mention of a customer. She knew he'd been chasing her clients away. Had heard the rumors and could tell by the way his eyes blazed that he was angry.

"I'm here on business, actually," he said tightly.

A muscle twitched in his jaw giving away his tension.

"Oh? And what business is that? Your next payment isn't due until the end of the month? That's still a week away."

She wondered if he'd seen the saddlebag Logan had brought into her kitchen. She'd moved it off the table and placed it in the corner behind the table out of the way. If he'd glanced down at the floor behind the table, he would have seen it. Surely, he'd seen Logan's black leather jacket. She couldn't remember where he'd left it. And had his two friends left anything of theirs lying around? How was she going to explain that? Like it was his business? She'd tell him that straight out if he asked.

Without waiting for an answer, she walked over to her dresser grabbed her brush and started brushing her hair. If he thought it odd, she hadn't washed the top of her hair while she'd been taking a bath, he didn't mention it. Perhaps it was damp enough from all that splashing around during their foot sex? She tensed as his eyes strayed to the closed bathroom door. Thankfully, though, he didn't move toward it.

"There was a train robbery over in Parkway," he said.

Parkway was a city south along the quickly crumbling highway going through an area that had once been called Banff National Park. City and town names used before the Catastrophe were being changed as survivors took over. There were so many changes, she hadn't bothered to keep track any longer.

"Oh? So that's the one that's thirty or so miles north of here?"

"Thirty-five miles south, actually."

"Anyone hurt?" she asked as she kept brushing her strands and stared at him in the mirror. She noticed how his gaze drifted from the closed bathroom door to her face as she asked that question. Good. Now all she needed to do was keep his attention focused on her and hopefully he wouldn't ask why the door was shut.

"One of the guards was wounded. Nothing serious."

"Well, that's a good thing. So, what brings you here?"

She leaned over allowing the top part of her robe to fall open as she brushed her hair from underneath. Hopefully, he'd be distracted by a good look at her breasts to forget why he'd come. Yeah right.

Linus cleared his throat, but his gaze remained on the curves of her exposed breasts.

"T...The Durango Gang...was responsible. They...uh...split up...um... into groups of three men each."

A blade of uneasiness swept through her. Okay so she didn't have to do the math regarding having three men on her property.

"They...uh...ride horses." He cleared his throat again and shifted uneasily on his feet.

Lovely, Logan had come with a horse. What about the other two? She hadn't seen any, but they could have put their horses in the barn before they'd even come into the house to announce their arrival.

"Doesn't everybody ride horses these days? Gas prices being the way they are."

Gosh, she hoped he didn't hear the loud thumps of her heart.

Had he checked the barn? No, he would be jumpy or out of character if he'd investigated and seen a strange horse or horses. Or, for that matter, if he'd seen Cassidy and Spencer. And if those two had seen the sheriff approaching surely, they would have sounded the alarm. So, that probably meant the sheriff didn't know she had company and Spencer and Cassidy may not know.

Great scenario if the two decided to announce their arrival in her farmhouse with this guy here. If they were the outlaws, there was a potential for a shootout here. She needed to get him out of here and fast.

Her blood froze at his next words.

"I...um noticed...two sets of horse tracks about a mile from here. A single set...uh...two miles up the road. All three sets...um... disappeared into the river that runs directly through your land. Um...did you see anyone?"

Teyla laughed, hoping it didn't sound as forced and nervous as it sounded to her.

"With most of the world's population wiped out, I've seen maybe one stranger since the Catastrophe." Too bad you didn't get wiped out too, she added silently. Life would have been a whole lot easier if he had literally been snuffed to dust.

"I'm afraid you've come to the wrong place," she continued. "If you're looking for three men sheriff, I only do one at a time and two a day. Keeps the doctor away."

She winked at him and the sheriff frowned and shifted restlessly. Obviously not comfortable with what she was saying.

Once again, he cleared his throat as she stopped brushing her hair and straightened up, the top part of her robe naturally covering her breasts again.

"I just want you to...um...to be careful. You being here all alone and everything. People with self-sustainable farms are being killed outright and their homes taken."

Great. Was that a threat?

Teyla steadied her nerves and placed her handbrush onto the letters Dr. Liz had sent regarding Logan and his two friends, then she slipped her hand into her robe pocket, quickly withdrawing the item she kept there. It was her backup gun.

One of many that she'd found while pillaging through neighboring homes after the Catastrophe. Homes where her friends had once lived, before her friends too had disintegrated. No ammo for this gun, but hey, he didn't need to know that, now did he.

His pale blue eyes widened in surprise and his long moustache twitched nervously when she pulled out her gun. Bubbles of excitement burst inside her as he took a couple of steps backward. If the deep valley of her exposed breasts hadn't fully caught his attention, well, her small derringer certainly did.

"Easy with that gun, Teyla" he sputtered.

"I'm just showing you I can take care of myself. Now if you don't mind, I really must get ready for my next customer. Can I show you out?" She purposely pointed the gun at him. He took another couple of steps backward.

"Easy with that gun. It might go off."

"Oh, it'll only go off, if I want it to," she replied, forcing a casualness into her voice that she didn't feel.

She strolled past him and out of her bedroom, thankful to hear his footsteps following behind. She sighed in relief to find he'd left the kitchen door wide open to the point where it hid the area where Logan's black leather jacket would be hanging. Good. He hadn't seen the jacket.

A renewed sense of urgency slashed through her as she stopped at the kitchen front door, her hand on the doorknob, pushing the door open even more, making double sure Logan's jacket remained hidden. She needed to get rid of Linus in case Spencer, Logan and Cassidy were the men he was looking for.

It was at that moment she realized she may just have to shoot this man if any of the others decided to make an appearance. But could she murder someone? And why was she entertaining the idea of shooting this self-proclaimed lawman if the three men were fugitives?

A tremor of unease ripped through her at her next thought.

The Durango Gang were notorious for stealing from the rich and giving to the poor. Until now she'd thought those types of men were ruthless. But the tender, possessive, and thoughtful ways Logan and the other two, had treated her, threw the idea of them being ruthless right out the window.

"Maybe you should tell me their descriptions? Just in case?" she spoke, daring to keep him here a moment longer. For all she knew she could have just slept with three ruthless bank robbers. Maybe even killers?

A shot of adrenaline zipped through her at the thought she may have experienced the most exquisite sex in her life with outlaws.

Another idea rocked her.

What if they decided she was a loose end that needed to be tied up? That they had no choice but to kill her? Maybe she should tell the sheriff the potential robbers were in her home? That two of them were outside, maybe even waiting to ambush him and that one was hiding in her very own bathroom?

Logan couldn't make out what Teyla and the intruder were saying, no matter how hard he listened.

Damn her! Why had she shut the door? She could have at least left it open a crack. Was she at this moment, turning him in? Had the others been caught? What was happening out there?

It had grown quiet out there. Too quiet. His uneasiness slipped up several notches.

Where had everyone gone? From his vantage point in the tub, he eyed the bathroom window and tried to see past the frilly white lace curtains. But the window was too small and he was too far down. He could only see the blue sky. Disappointment rocked him.

His gaze dropped to the bathroom floor, to the shattered glass and where he'd left his jeans. Had the intruder been able to see the glass and his pants when Teyla had stepped out into the bedroom? Or before that when he'd inadvertently left the door slightly ajar? Hopefully if he had seen, he may think she had a customer in here with her. Unless, whoever was out there knew about Spencer and Cassidy.

Where the hell was she? Where were Cassidy and Spencer? Damn their hides.

Another thought shot through him. Maybe the newcomer was another customer?

Logan did not like the gut twisting way he was feeling at thinking another customer had shown up. Maybe she was servicing him right now? Maybe she'd taken him upstairs into one of her other bedrooms?

His grip on the neck of the wine bottle tightened to the point where his wrist and fingers actually hurt. He loosened his grip and forced his breaths to slow down. Tried to not imagine her with strange men.

She better not be with another guy. Man, he'd known her for such a brief time and he was already dictating who she could or could not see? Not good, my man. Not good at all.

Maybe he should just go out there and see what was going on? Take what belonged to him and smash the bottle over the bastard's head. Better yet get his gun and shoot, ask questions later.

Why had he left his gun out of his sight? He never did that.

The bathroom door burst inward totally catching him off guard. But he reacted quickly, lifting the bottle. He was just about to bring it down on the edge of the bathtub, in order to break it and go after the intruder, when he stopped, realizing who had entered.

"Teyla," he whispered.

The look of surprise and shock on her face had him holding back another string of curses as he quickly got out of the tub.

"He's gone. But I don't know where your friends are. I hope they're okay."

Logan stepped around the broken glass and raced to the bathroom window just in time to see a man hop into a black car and drive away. No signs of his partners.

"They're big boys. They can take care of themselves." Yeah, he was worried, but if something had happened to them, surely this guy wouldn't leave just like he had.

"Who was he?" Another customer, he asked silently.

"He's the law around here."

Great. Just great.

"Does he drop by often?" he asked a little too gruffly as he swept his jeans off the floor and hurriedly stepped into them.

The last thing they needed was the law visiting her on a damned regular basis. He wanted to ask her if she serviced him too but he bit back that bitter question, as he noticed she was hesitating in answering.

She averted her gaze and worried her bottom lip. Okay, not a good sign when she did those things and not answer his question.

Up until this guy had shown up, she'd been very cooperative. That her attitude had suddenly changed irritated him and he grabbed her arm a bit too roughly. Immense guilt slammed through him at the look of surprise and fear slashing across her face.

"I didn't tell him anything," she snapped and tried to pull her arm from his grasp.

Anger flared in her pretty eyes and he cursed himself for scaring her and forced himself to calm down.

"I didn't ask that question, Teyla."

"I said he's the law. He doesn't need an invitation. He drops by whenever he feels like it."

Whenever he feels like it? Irritation snapped through him like a live wire.

Chill, Logan. Chill. The guys said she didn't sleep with him. He needed to relax and remember that.

The jovial sounds of his friends' voices outside made Logan realize they probably didn't have a clue they'd just had a visitor.

"Get dressed. Wear something pretty. I need to talk to the others," he told her and ignored the pout on her mouth. A mouth he wanted to kiss and make love to.

Damn, but he sure did have it bad for her, didn't he?

He didn't miss the pink flush in her cheeks or the sultry sparkle in her eyes. Maybe she wanted another ménage?

Oh shit. He needed to get away from her before he took her up against the bathroom wall or before he fell head over heels in love with the woman. He left the bathroom and rushed to the bedside table.

Opening the drawer, he ignored the condoms and lifted out the gun he'd placed in there earlier.

Familiar relief at having his gun back in his grasp enveloped him, but despite the relief his heart hammered insanely against his chest as he realized exactly how dangerous the situation had been. The law had come calling and the boys had been absent. Not to mention he'd been so jealous; he'd almost turned on her.

Yup, he was crazy. That cop could come back. Could have caught him literally with his pants down. Put a bullet into him.

He swore softly and headed outside.

Tugging her robe around her, Teyla took a shuddering breath and gazed at herself in the mirror. Sizzling shimmers scampered up and down her back. She looked...well, she looked erotic.

Her hair was a gorgeous mess, her mouth looked plump and red from kissing and her eyes seemed so bright, someone might think she had a fever.

Opening her robe, she gazed at her nude body. It even looked different. Voluptuous. Her breasts appeared huge, felt swollen. Her nipples were pert and red from their touches. And the area between her thighs and her ass throbbed intensely with a need she'd not felt before.

She wanted to be taken by Logan again. Wanted to experience another ménage. But these men could be dangerous if what the sheriff had said was true. The exorbitant amount of money they were paying her for her services proved to her they were into something illegal. And Logan's uneasy reaction when she'd told him the law had been here pretty much confirmed he was part of that Durango gang.

Oh crap. Wasn't that just her rotten luck? Falling for a guy who was a desperado. A guy, who, if caught by the law, would swing by the neck until he was dead.

These days, despite a self-appointed sheriff, there really wasn't any sort of legal justice. It was vigilantism all the way around. A posse grabbed their suspects and dished out the punishment as they saw fit.

Robbers and killers were treated alike. Hanged by the neck until dead. Which left her with the question what should she do now?

Up until now they hadn't given her a reason to be afraid of them. They'd been quite pleasurable. Kind.

Studs.

If they'd wanted to harm her, they would have done that, wouldn't they? And her instincts would have told her to beware.

Besides, her friend, Dr. Elizabeth, had said they could be trusted in that note she'd sent with Logan. It was her handwriting, and her perfume splashing from the note, so there wasn't any doubt about who had written it. And her friend wouldn't have joked about sizes if she'd been under pressure to write out a note for Teyla.

Oh, for Pete's sakes, if they were dangerous to her, they would have ridden in and taken her against her will, and not gone to all this trouble of coming with notes and paying her. Logan wouldn't have been so damned nice to her and everything.

No, he wasn't a danger. She wasn't a judge on why he would run with the Durango Gang *if* he were at all. Besides, what they did was none of her business.

Right?

Right! She firmly told herself.

Besides, she was just doing her job. Being a Pleasure Girl. No one could judge her for doing her job and who was *she* to judge them?

Wear something pretty, Logan had said. Exactly what did he mean by that? Pretty like in a dress she'd wear to a cocktail party? Like that wasn't happening since she didn't attend parties. Or did he want her to dress sexy like she wanted to have sex with three men again.

Oh God, she had to be too stupid to live to actually be entertaining thoughts of more sex with potential outlaws.

Teyla rolled her eyes and headed back into her bedroom.

Yep, obviously she was too stupid to live because that's exactly what she wanted.

"You two were what?" Logan exploded. He couldn't believe his ears.

"Fixing the door to her greenhouse out behind the barn. We tended to the horses and then took a walk out back, saw some work needed doing and did it," Spencer said, eying Logan as if he had two heads for even asking him to repeat what he'd just said.

Holy crap! They hadn't been here more than a few hours and they were already domesticated.

"Why? What's wrong?" Cassidy asked as he came up behind Spencer, a frown of concern zipping across his face.

His gaze dropped to between Logan's thighs to where Logan was already hard again.

"Not that it looks like there is anything wrong down south," he winked.

"Cop was here."

Well, that certainly took the air out of both men's sails, didn't it? He took immense satisfaction in their sudden sobering looks as both men went for their guns. Their relaxed gazes snapped to the look of the hunted and Logan instantly felt better.

This was the way they were supposed to be. All three of them. On guard, ready to protect each other and cover each other's backs, not fixing up a rundown farm.

But wasn't that exactly what he'd wanted to do when he'd sat up on that hillside gazing down at Teyla's rundown farm nestled snugly in the valley? Yeah, he had felt exactly that way. Damned domesticated.

Hanging out with Teyla made them forget the fact they were fugitives. Wanted men. And he knew they'd die shooting to prevent themselves from getting hanged by the neck compliments of a vigilante law.

"What the hell happened?" they both asked at the same time and crowded in around Logan. Their guns were now drawn, their backs against each other as if expecting shots to be fired at any second.

Good, he'd spooked them. This is the way they needed to be.

Alert. Ready for trouble.

Not working a freaking farm and sexing the cutest woman he'd come across in one hell of a long time.

"He's gone. Teyla got rid of him. She doesn't know when he'll be back, and as we know any type of law is unpredictable."

Both men seemed to relax, but the familiar tension remained. It sparkled between the three of them reminding them of the close call.

"You sure she handled it okay?" *Like can we stay longer?* Can we have sex with her individually? Were pretty much the messages Logan was reading from Cassidy's question and the eager look on both men's faces as they awaited his answer.

"It needs to be all three of us together or just me. She's never done this ménage stuff before. I don't want us scaring her off and having her change her mind."

Which, if he really thought about it, was what she'd originally agreed to. Him and his two friends. He hadn't mentioned for her to service them individually...had he?

Cassidy frowned. "I thought-" his words were cut off by a sharp jab to his ribs, compliments of Spencer, who of course wanted some one on one time with Teyla.

"Logan set it up this time. If that's what the lady says, that's the way it will be. You know the rules. Always listen to the lady's wishes. Now, let's get washed up and get started on supper," Cassidy replied.

Spencer muttered his disappointment beneath his breath, turned, and strode toward the red water pump fifty yards away. Cassidy stayed; his intense gaze fixed on Logan. The guy was studying Logan as if he were some curious insect or something.

"What gives with the chick? Last night you said she was in agreement with us three doing her. That also meant some one on one, right? Who changed their mind? Her? Or you? Are you sweet on her?"

Who wouldn't be?

"She's tired. I don't want to push her." Damned if he was going to admit he wanted the woman within his sight all the time. Hell, who is he kidding? He wanted her first. Then he would share her.

"It's what ladies do. They change their minds," Logan said.

"Uh huh, if you say so, Logan. We'll keep our hands off until you say so. Just don't get too involved. You know the rules," he warned.

Too late, my man. He wanted to tell Cassidy exactly that, but he kept his big mouth shut. They'd leave sometime tomorrow as planned and once he was out of here and away from her, he'd forget her and they would rejoin the Durango Gang and could continue on with their crusade.

"Just keep your eyes open for anything suspicious," he told Cassidy and headed back to the farm. He could hardly wait to see her again.

Oh man, he was so screwed.

Chapter Nine

Teyla tensed when she heard Logan's heavy footsteps come up the stairs and across the wooden veranda. She'd put on the sexiest dress she owned. She'd worn it only once, to a fundraiser local farmers were throwing to raise cash for a couple who were about to lose their farm due to foreclosure.

Max, bless his soul, had volunteered her services in the kissing booth the farmers had set up at the fair. Her husband insisted she look sexy and had brought the dress home for her.

She had to admit she'd thinned since last wearing it several years ago, but the black clingy halter top really enhanced her breasts, and the bottom half was a billowy ankle length ball gown.

That she stood in her kitchen wearing the dress, in her bare feet, peeling carrots for the men's supper was odd. But hey, she was being paid big bucks to follow his orders so, if he wanted her wearing something pretty, then that's what she would do. She just hoped Logan liked the dress.

Her heart fluttered as the screen door creaked open. She swallowed as his footsteps halted abruptly. When he didn't come inside, she dared a look over her shoulder and her insides went all wobbly at his primal gaze. Like he was the predator and she was his for the taking.

He let out a slow whistle and nodded his head.

"Nice. Very nice," he said softly, his voice drenched with approval.

She swallowed and returned her attention to peeling the carrots, her heart pounding with wicked abandon as he let the screen door shut behind him. He sauntered behind her and she inhaled softly as he is hot palms nestled on her hips, his face nuzzling her neck, the sharp bristles of his shadow rubbing erotically against her skin.

"You look so delicious I could just eat you up," he muttered. "Keep peeling those carrots. I want to watch."

"First a foot fetish and now a peeling fetish?" She teased.

"Not a peeling fetish. A certain woman fetish."

Her? Oh my.

"A man of many talents."

She grinned and kept peeling while he nuzzled her neck. She could definitely feel the hard bulge of his cock as he ground against her backside. It was an erotic rhythm. Sultry, full of promise that she would receive a hot evening of sex with him.

"How are the guys?" she asked.

Just mentioning them made her quiver as she remembered the wild sex in the living room. Oh dear, her cheeks were warming up again. Not good.

She refocused her thoughts to what she'd noticed earlier when she'd watched from the window as Logan had joined the other two in the yard.

As Logan had talked with them, she'd noticed the two men's easy-going stances change to instant tension and alert.

Obviously, they hadn't seen the sheriff until they'd been told he'd been here.

"They'll be in after washing up, I'm sure."

He leaned his lower half against her, pressing his cock against her ass much in the same way he'd done yesterday evening. She trembled as he sucked her left ear lobe into his mouth.

"Woah, there, big boy," she breathed.

Gosh, the intoxicating way his tongue licked her flesh had her dropping the paring knife again. It clattered to the counter.

She moaned, giving up control and melting into the erotic sensations sweeping through her. Leaning back against him she thoroughly enjoying the way his hands tangled with hers and the seductive way he nibbled and sucked her lobe. Who knew a man's mouth could feel so erotic.

Suddenly he let go and drew away, his breathing harsh and raspy and that's when she heard the other men stomping up the stairs.

Bummer.

"To be continued later," he promised in a low voice, and stepped away from her, quickly taking a seat at the table.

Spencer and Cassidy were joking amiably as they entered. But when they saw her, Teyla read the fire flaring in their eyes. Saw their need for more sex.

Her pussy creamed. She swallowed, forced herself to look away and return to her carrots.

"Good evening, gentlemen, are you hungry?" She called out, trying really hard to act normal and ignore the insistent flare of heat hugging her cheeks and body as she dropped the carrots into the boiling water.

"Ravenous," Spencer chuckled.

"Starving," Cassidy growled.

By the low tone of their voices, she knew they weren't speaking about dinner but about her. Logan obviously picked up on it too.

"Since you boys are in such a domestic mood, why don't you both set the table?" he advised from his perch, obviously a bit irritated at the two of them being disturbed.

"Now that's an idea," Cassidy replied and before she knew it the two men were fighting over gathering the dinner plates from the nearby cupboard.

Cassidy won and he moved with a grace she'd not seen in a man before. He reminded her of a cougar quietly stalking his prey. As if sensing her watching him, he glanced at her and winked, before taking the plates and glasses back to the table.

Teyla's cheeks grew hotter as Spencer asked where he could find the utensils, his gaze snapping wildfire as he also gave her a longing look before reaching into the drawer she'd indicated. As he moved away, she blew out a tense and hot breath and remembered yet again how the three men had taken her earlier.

And now she was preparing dinner for them. She should be more embarrassed than this, shouldn't she? Having sex with three guys wasn't normal for her, so why was she so...well, calm wouldn't be the right word.

Excited. Aroused. Needy.

Wanting more ménages, sounded about right.

"They fixed the greenhouse door for you," Logan said. She heard amusement as well as pride in his voice at his announcement.

"Ah, come on, Log. We wanted it to be a surprise for her. We were going to show her after dinner," Spencer complained as he reached for an oil lamp on a nearby shelf and brought it down, readying it for later.

Teyla hadn't even realized it was already getting dark outside again.

My, oh, my, the day had gone by fast.

As she watched the two strangers setting the table, she once again warmed to the memories of what had transpired earlier with the four of them.

Her on the bed, naked, strange men touching her, massaging her breasts, her clit. Kissing her. Moving her into the living room. Having her ass impaled by Logan and being triple penetrated and all that naughty sex.

Oh my gosh, three men having sex with her. She just couldn't get over it!

And now all of them acting like one big happy family, setting the table. Except the entire time she watched the family scene unfolding, she became very aware of Logan's gaze on her. Very aware indeed.

Even from here at the counter she could smell him as she cut up more vegetables that she'd harvested from her greenhouse a couple of days ago. She tossed the carrots into the pot.

Logan smelled like sex and desperation and bubble bath.

Gosh, she couldn't believe she'd had foot sex in her bathtub, with bubbles and a man. Every time she looked at the tub, she'd think of their afternoon together. Mercy, it *was* getting so hot in here. With the back of her hand, she brushed away the whisper of perspiration blossoming across her forehead and looked up to find Logan still watching her.

The intensity of his gaze made her tummy do some wonderful little flip-flops and she wished she and Logan had met under other circumstances. Things would have been so different. Instead of being a pleasure girl to him he would have taken her out for coffee or dinner and a movie. Sex would have followed a little later on when the attraction could no longer be denied. Then the scorching ménages would have begun because it was obvious to her, he enjoyed sharing her.

She sighed and smiled at Logan, who in turn winked at her. Well, no use in dreaming about what could have been. Things just were.

Logan was impressed at the men's behavior toward Teyla. With other women who'd serviced them, Cassidy and Spencer had been their usual loud cheerful selves. But tonight, both men minded their manners. Calling her maám and politely asking each other to pass this or that.

By the time supper ended he couldn't stop himself from beaming or admitting to himself that his two partners in crime had never behaved better. Then all too soon reality came crashing in around Logan. He felt as if the weight of the world had once again settled on his shoulders when Spencer asked Teyla the question he knew should have been brought up much earlier. But once again they'd let their guards down while enjoying a home cooked meal.

"How did you manage to get rid of that guy who came snooping around this afternoon? Logan mentioned he was a cop or something? What did he want?"

Logan watched Teyla for her reaction. Her easy-going attitude changed immediately and she suddenly looked wary and he even caught a glimpse of that fear he'd seen slice across her face earlier when she'd first entered the bathroom after getting rid of their unwanted visitor.

Dammit. He'd forgotten that reaction. Why had the sheriff dropped in?

Logan had assumed he'd wanted servicing, but now with Teyla's sudden nervous attitude and the other two picking up on it, both of them frowning and glancing with puzzlement at Logan, he knew his next course of action. He gave them a quick nod of his head signaling them to clear out so he could be alone with Teyla.

"I'm up for a walk. How about you, Cass? You want to tag along?" Spencer asked.

"Yep, right behind you," Cassidy answered as he quickly followed Spencer to the door where they grabbed their jackets. The slam of the door behind them made Teyla visibly tense.

"Okay, so why was he here, if not for you?"

Her eyes widened at his question and she stood and began clearing the dishes.

"He was just checking in on me. That's all."

She was now worrying her lower lip, and he concluded she wasn't telling him the truth.

"You're lying." He may as well confront her on it right up front.

"That's awfully nice of you calling me a liar," she snapped and she slammed the dinner dishes into the sink. Whirling around, her eyes sparkled with irritation and anger.

"Why the sudden interest in what he wanted? It's not like you're the outlaws he's looking for, is it?"

Shit, that man *had* been looking for them. Son of a bitch. He needed to tell the guys.

He should tell her the truth too. Tell her what he and the others did. Why they were constantly on the run. Why they paid for their women instead of settling down with a nice chick like her.

Oh, come on, Logan. You're getting too sappy on this one, he scolded himself. She's a hooker. She sleeps with guys for living. That's her job. That's her only interest in you. Now get the answer out of her and start thinking of an exit strategy. If he were smart, he'd get the hell out tonight. Just in case this self-proclaimed law guy dropped in again, this time with a freaking posse.

He saw the indecision flare in her eyes. The hesitation. That inkling of fear again. Maybe even distrust?

He took a step toward her. Didn't like the way she frowned at him for doing so.

"I need to know, sweetheart." Oh man, that was a first. Calling one of the women who'd serviced him, sweetheart.

"He said the Durango gang was around. He said they did a railroad robbery a few days ago. That the posse discovered the gang had split into three groups and one group was trailed to the next town over. He also picked up horse tracks which disappeared into the river that comes through my property so he came over to warn me to be careful."

"And you didn't mention we were here?"

"I told him I was waiting for my next customer and that customer wouldn't appreciate him being here. He wants me, but he gets turned off whenever I mention other men."

"I bet," he growled in agreement as irritation slammed through him at the idea of other men being here with her.

He noticed a wisp of a smile reach her lips and it seemed like she was pleased at what he'd said. Pleased that he was jealous.

Suddenly the sweet rush of wanting to have sex with her again took hold. He wanted to bury himself deep inside her and possess her. Brand her as his. Wanted to make sure she never forgot him and make sure she never fell into any other man's arms again.

Oh yeah, he was drowning in her sparkling eyes. His cock was getting too hard for comfort. He needed to get away from her before he splayed her out on the kitchen table and took her again.

"I need to check on the guys."

"Want company?" she asked, a little shyly. So cute. Too cute.

He sighed softly as indecision gripped him. He needed to make plans with the guys. Needed to keep a guard out so the other two could take her.

Oh man, he needed to stop thinking about sex. About her.

Take her for a walk, you idiot. Treat her like a woman. Not a hooker.

Oh hell, she was a woman. Fine and delicate as lace. Sweet as sin.

He relaxed his roiling emotions and forced himself to smile. Yeah, he wanted her company. Didn't want to be away from her.

Reaching out his hand, he took hers, loving the warmth and strength of her fingers as they intertwined with his.

Oh yeah, this feels too good.

"He won't be back if that's what has you worried. He said he was getting a posse together and heading out to pick up their trail," she said.

There was quietness in her tone and he could read the truth in her eyes. He knew she wasn't lying.

Their trail, she'd said. Not your trail. Hell, yeah, he really should tell her the truth. He could trust her, especially if Dr. Elizabeth had sent him here. They wouldn't be coming this way again. He'd covered his trail and he knew Cassidy and Spencer would have covered theirs too. They made it a habit of always hiding their tracks by heading to a river or a creek and when they came out, they took immense time making sure there was no sign of where they exited. They would be safe. For now.

"Let's go and check out what they did with your greenhouse door."

She nodded and before they left the farmhouse, he grabbed her cardigan and helped her into it. Evenings were cold and he wanted her to stay warm and safe. The safe part he couldn't guarantee, but he could keep her warm while he was here.

Taking her hand again, they stepped outside. From the porch, they had a great vantage point of the setting sun perched on top of one of the nearby snowcapped mountains. The sun was a gold ball and as it descended behind the mountain, it cast an eerie golden hue over the buildings and the yellow grasslands. He knew he'd make an excellent target standing out on the porch if someone was aiming at him. But hell, he wanted to be here with her and watch the sunset. It just felt so normal.

"Are you and the guys the ones they're looking for?" She asked in a quiet whisper as if not wanting to disturb the beautiful scenery as they stood at the railing.

With the blazing glow of setting sun splashing gold against her face he could see the highlights of auburn flicker in her eyes and streaking her bangs. She looked so damn pretty he just couldn't get over it. How some guy hadn't snatched her up before now was a mystery. It pretty much said guys around these parts were nuts.

"And if I said that we are running from vigilantes and the law, would it change anything?" he asked.

She lowered her gaze and he caught a split-second of disappointment, maybe even devastation, but then she lifted her chin with defiance and her eyes fixed on him with a smoky look that told him it didn't really matter.

"I just need to know one thing," she said with a delicate softness.

"What's that?"

"Why are you running with the Durango gang?"

Why? Good question.

He winced as a multitude of emotions shot through him. Anger. Loss. Despair.

Fighting the people who lined their pockets on the misery and desperation of others really wasn't his business. But after losing his daughters, his wife, and his life, he'd needed a reason to stay alive. How did he explain that to her?

"Let's just say it's something I needed to do."

She smiled, seemingly satisfied with his vague answer.

"Come on, let's go see what they did." He tugged her hand and was pleased she easily followed.

Chapter Ten

He led her behind the barn to the glass greenhouse. It was a large building, sheltered from the north by the barn. The greenhouse was about fifty feet long by about forty feet wide. Only the southern exposure consisted of glass panes. Some panes were broken and patched haphazardly with plastic sheets.

"They did a wonderful job with the door," she exclaimed as she let go of his hand and ran to the greenhouse. She examined the leather strips, which the guys had nailed to the door and the frame of the building.

"They made hinges out of the leather!" she gushed. "The old rusty metal hinges snapped in two and right off a few weeks back during a really bad windstorm when I accidentally left the door ajar one time. I didn't have any replacements. They cost too much in town so I just moved the door back and forth. And it was always so heavy. Sometimes I was so tired I couldn't move it into place as best as it should have and the building lost lots of heat."

He inspected their handiwork and felt proud at how tight the door fit the frame and the fact they'd screwed in a heavy-duty leather loop that would fit over a long nail and would help keep the door closed. The door was a sheet of heavy-duty glass framed by solid oak and certainly did look heavy. Too heavy for a pretty woman.

Oh, man, she needed help around here. He could clearly see that. She needed someone to slap some red paint on the barn. Fill in the cracks of the foundation in the buildings. Replace the shingles fluttering off the roof of the farmhouse.

She needed a man around here to help her run the place. To protect her from creeps like that banker-sheriff who one day wouldn't take no for an answer from her.

She needed a man, like himself?

He jolted at that thought and cursed silently to himself. He wasn't through with his revenge. Not yet. Maybe not ever.

She opened the greenhouse door with ease and ushered him inside. It smelled of earth and flowers in here. It smelled normal.

They stopped just inside the door where she reached for an oil lamp hanging on a post. She struck a match from a match box she unwrapped from a plastic encasing and in an instant a buttery glow from the lamp fell across her face.

Her eyes were twinkling with pride as she led him down the main aisle. There were many rows filled with wooden boxes lining both sides of the aisle. Boxes filled with dirt. Some, to his surprise, had little green sprouts shooting up. Other boxes were bare of dirt or had dirt but no plants. While other boxes contained plants in various stages of growth. He recognized carrot tops and spinach. One box was filled with Boston lettuce. Other boxes he didn't know what was growing.

But it all looked so healthy and he felt pride sift through him that this woman wasn't as helpless out here as he'd thought.

"Impressive," he commented as the warmth of the room caressed his face while he looked around.

The floor was dirt and instantly he knew she'd be better off with a wooden floor with a couple of inches of Styrofoam insulation beneath the floorboards. The insulation would certainly improve the heat possibilities.

He was surprised to hear the buzzing of bees nearby and noticed several of them hugging yellow flowers on what looked like tomato plants. In one corner he noticed a couple of white painted wooden boxes and a bee buzzing there as well.

Amazing.

"My husband and I put the greenhouse together from a kit, shortly after we moved here."

Pride echoed in her voice. He could tell she missed her husband and that familiar fluttering of jealousy zipped through him again. Cripes, he appeared to be jealous of a dead man.

"Over here is my prize possession." Happiness bubbled through her voice and sweet laugh lines whispered along the sides of her eyes as she led him to a box laden with dirt and plants topped with large white flowers. Each flower had three white petals and three large green leaves.

Shock and surprise exploded through him.

"Trilliums? Where did you get them?" Wow, he hadn't seen trilliums since before the Catastrophe!

"I dug up bulbs a couple of years ago. I remembered I had some in planters out back. When they didn't sprout, I dug them up and transplanted them in here. I know it takes up space for something that would be useful like turnips or carrots-"

He stopped her talking by placing a finger on her warm lips. Man, he was acquiring a habit of doing that, wasn't he?

"I'm babbling, aren't I?" she said against his finger.

"You don't need to explain to me why you need flowers. It's obvious."

Her eyes widened in question.

"Because you don't have a man who brings you flowers," he explained and loved the way her eyes smiled at him. She liked his teasing. He liked her.

Her lips moved sweetly against his finger as she smiled.

I'll be that man, he silently said in his mind. He really should say it aloud. He was tempted to say it, but that freaking green northern lights thing began flashing across the glass panes of the greenhouse, distracting him.

You'd think he'd have gotten used to those lights by now, but sometimes they just threw off his concentration. Or more likely he was using the areola borealis as an excuse to not think about how he really wanted to be the one to bring her flowers every morning? Because he suddenly ached to do just that.

To bring her flowers and tell her how much he loved those crinkles at the sides of her eyes when she smiled.

"What's got you all quiet suddenly? What are you thinking?" she asked softly.

That I want to settle down here with you. The thought of doing that sent an ache so severe shooting through him it literally felt like a punch to his stomach.

"What's wrong?" she asked and to his surprise she stabbed her warm tongue against the finger he still held against her lips.

"Nothing's wrong, baby. Show me the rest of the greenhouse. Like how do you manage to keep it so warm in here at night?"

He dropped his hand and looked around the building. Noticed several barrels lining the west wall.

"Solar panels on top of the roof keep the water in the barrels warm. At night, the warmth evaporates from the barrels and keeps the air warm and moist. The rest of the place is insulated. I'm saving up for materials to put in a floor that can produce radiant heat. Then I can grow produce that can't stand the cold, like berries. God, what I wouldn't give for strawberry shortcake." She grinned and continued. "When I start selling produce, I won't charge and arm and a leg...hmm, I should rephrase that, shouldn't I? I'm not into eating humans..."

She let her words trail off and her cheeks flushed pink as she obviously remembered taking Cassidy's cock in her mouth earlier today and Logan yesterday. Just remembering how nice and tight she sucked, had him hardening again.

"I'm definitely into feet," she said huskily, referring to their foot fucking in the bathtub. Oh yeah, he was into feet too.

"And I might be into fingers, too," she teased.

She reached down and lifted his hand to her face, maneuvering his forefinger to her mouth as he'd done only moments before. She licked his finger in a sultry way and her eyelids drooped with arousal.

Shit. Sexy kitten wasn't she. He swallowed and his cock throbbed even more.

He watched as she curled her tongue around his finger and slipped the tip into her mouth. She sucked gently.

Oh man, the pressure was too sweet. That she was initiating this impromptu sexual escapade made him ponder that maybe she wanted more sex from him as opposed to because he was paying for it? There was a significant difference between the two scenarios.

The latter idea of her wanting sex made his blood pressure roar. Made him struggle to draw breath into his lungs. Just thinking that she could be his, had him wondering if he had died and maybe gone to heaven.

He smiled and placed a second finger against her velvety lower lip. She licked it and he dipped his fingers inside her mouth, loving the way her warm tongue curled against both his fingers. Yeah, the way her eyes twinkled happily as she licked him was really firing his blood and a weird thought flared through him. The thought that maybe she really liked him.

Something changed in him the moment she licked his fingers. Something so subtle, she almost missed it. Suddenly she had the feeling he didn't want to leave here. But that idea was ridiculous. Wasn't it?

Yes, it was insane. She'd only met him yesterday. She knew next to nothing about him. She was being silly. And romantic. And stupid.

Despite those thoughts though, she felt sexy. Really truly sexy and a wicked need burst through her. She wanted Logan and the other two men to make love to her again. But since Logan was here now, she wanted him. Right here. But first...

"Stay here. I'll be back in a second," she ordered.

She left him standing there and headed back toward the front door. Up on a shelf she found her small radio and flicked it on. Despite the world having gone mad, a couple of stations had managed to keep pumping out the news and music. She rarely used the radio because she preferred not to listen to the news. Or music. News was just bad all the way around and music just reminded her of the old days. Days that were gone forever.

Goosebumps zipped up her arms as the soft music drifted through the warm greenhouse air. It was a slow song. Beautiful lyrics. A song about the sun and walking in fields of gold.

Instead of the music making her feel sad, to her amazement happiness simmered through her and so did a glimmer of hope.

Maybe, just maybe Logan would come back again? Yeah, she could handle anything if she knew he was coming back.

When she returned to him, she found him sitting cross legged on one of the table boxes filled with dirt. Thankfully, he'd picked one to sit on that she hadn't seeded yet.

She wanted to ask him if he was coming back to her but decided she really didn't want to know the answer. Not yet. Just in case he said no.

As the music drifted through the greenhouse, he stared at her. Really stared. His gaze was wild, his body tense and she knew he wanted sex too. As he watched her, she began to sway her hips to the music and smiled at him.

He grinned back and, in that smile, she saw the primitive need boiling inside him. Intense desire flared inside her and she felt sultry and sexy and, well, as if she belonged only to him.

Moving her hips in a sensual rhythm, she reached up and stabbed her hands through her hair, letting the strands trail through her fingers like a waterfall. He licked his lips as he watched her.

Unhurriedly, erotically, she untied the sash to her cardigan and slowly unbuttoned the garment. Keeping her eyes glued to him, she let the cardigan slip off her shoulders. It dropped to the floor. Now she only wore her shoes and that black halter dress her husband had given her.

Of course, his gaze zeroed right onto her breasts as they pushed boldly against the material. She shivered at the sight of the tip of his tongue peeking out from between his lips and the soft music didn't drown the sound of his heavy breathing or the loud excited thumping of her heart. She kept swaying to the music and as she did so, she slipped out of her shoes.

She continued to dance for him, her bare feet feeling a bit chilled on the cold ground, but his untamed gaze as he watched her kept the rest of her nice and toasty. She brought her hands up to her breasts, cupping them, offering them to him. His Adams apple bobbed as he swallowed. She watched his lips move as he swore softly. He was holding himself back. Maybe making it sweeter by doing that? It certainly made it sweeter for her as her anticipation increased and her desires for him became barely restrained.

She closed her eyes, melting into the music. Another song now. A faster beat. A song about a beautiful day and not letting it get away. About the heart being in bloom and going to another place.

Oh yes, her heart was in bloom. She was feeling something for this man she'd never felt before. A man who'd easily shared her with two of his friends. A man who looked at her with such desire and such need she just wanted to be in his arms forever.

Oh God, she was going to lose him, wasn't she? No, don't think about it, Teyla. Don't even go there.

Suddenly a pair of hands swept around her waist, hot brands digging into her flesh and her bare feet left the ground. His powerful scent wrapped around her, drugging her, intoxicating her. He lifted her higher.

"Shh, baby. I want you bad. Really bad." Logan whispered against her ear.

He set her upon the table he'd just been sitting on and she gasped in both surprise and shock and then excitement as he ripped the dress all the way down the front, to the hem. He ripped harder and that gave way too. He pushed the ragged material aside allowing the humid greenhouse air to sweep against her bare breasts and her pussy. His hands settled on her knees. He opened her wide. Spread her thighs for him. He moved in between her widespread legs, his hands on her thighs.

Wrapping her arms around his neck, she held him tight and his mouth locked onto hers like a heat seeking missile, his lips hard and demanding. She felt his muscles bulge beneath her arms as he let go of her thighs. A second later she heard the zipper on his pants lowering. Then heard the rip of foil. A condom. My gosh, was this guy prepared or what?

And if he were kissing her, how could he put on the condom? Oh, who cared! She almost lost herself in the anticipation of wanting him. Almost told him there was no need for a condom, but she didn't want to chance a baby. Not out here all by herself. But having his baby would be so perfect.

No! Stop! She had to be responsible. She had to be!

She broke the kiss; her breasts heaving as she caught her breath and watched him roll on the condom.

When he finished, she grabbed his velvet-steel encased cock and brought him into her. She was soaked and he entered her vagina with relative ease, impaling her to the hilt. He withdrew and thrust into her again, bringing a fever churning through her. She drew his head closer, kissed him. He opened his mouth to her and she plunged her tongue into it, boldly dueling with his tongue, exploring every crevice, touching ever inch, committing him to memory.

He groaned, cupped her breasts and squeezed. He withdrew his cock and thrust into her again. She arched against him, accepting his cock. Accepting his needs. Him.

As the music drifted through the air, his thrusts became faster, and the tension built inside her. Every stroke into her snapped her closer to that land of pleasure she was so getting hooked on since he'd been here.

Her orgasm built and hit her with a fury she'd never known before. Sensations pummeled her. Sheer pleasure pierced her and she kept keening as he rocked his hips and powered his cock in and out in a frenzied, exotic rhythm.

She convulsed and gasped and loved it. Her climax was long and explosive and finally he groaned and came right along with her.

When they came down together, he kept his cock buried inside her as he held her while the violent tremors ebbed through her vagina. His embrace was wonderful and soothing and before long she realized he was talking to her in soft tones, telling her that the other two men wanted to take her too.

"I want to watch them take you," he whispered against her throat and he was kissing her there then licking behind her earlobe and his hands were settling on her waist again.

Those two hot brands were firm and confident against her flesh. As if he knew she would accept more sex. And she knew she would. She wanted him to watch her be taken by another man.

Other men.

God, she was creaming at the thought of it. She had to be insane. Was she?

Just then she heard a noise and her eyes snapped open and as she looked over Logan's shoulder, she spied Cassidy and Spencer standing not more than ten feet away. Now it made sense what he'd just said about wanting to watch the other two take her.

They stared at her with lust in their eyes and shivers of excitement ripped through her. She noticed Cassidy holding the tube of lube and Spencer holding a box of condoms and a blanket from her house. Oh God, it looked like she was in for a long night.

Suddenly she became so aware of all three men. Everything else seemed to shift into the background. The music, the green plants in the various boxes surrounding them, even the aurora borealis that flickered green overhead through the greenhouse glass panes.

Nothing else existed. Just her sitting here on the cool packed earth of the table box and Logan. And Cassidy and Spencer.

Logan stopped kissing her and lifted her off the table. Her legs trembled from the after sex and she could smell herself. Smell her arousal as it floated through the air.

Logan held her hand as they watched Cassidy open the blanket and lay it upon a wide-open space in the middle of her greenhouse. Her breathing grew faster as the two undressed. She realized that this was the first time she could fully see Spencer and Cassidy's cocks and boy they were big. So big that she felt all warm and tingly at the idea they would be making love to her soon.

Right here. Right now.

Her mouth became dry as Logan led her onto the middle of the blanket. She recognized it as one that she kept on the couch in the living room. A knitted blanket that she'd once liked to cuddle up with in her other life when she'd sit in front of the warm flickering living room fireplace at night waiting for her late husband to come home from working in the fields.

But there was no more husband and oddly enough she didn't feel the least bit sad this time because she had Logan. And his two friends.

Friends who wanted to have sex with her. And she wanted them to. Wanted to lose herself in the pleasure and simply forget everything.

Logan gave her hand a squeeze before letting go and stepping away leaving her there, alone with the two strangers. He drifted off into the darkness and she could hear him breathing back there somewhere. Could imagine him watching them. Stroking himself. Pleasuring himself. Holding his cock in his hands. Maybe squeezing his large swollen sac.

Sweet mercy, she was shivering again. Trembling as the two naked men reached out and began touching her arms with feather light touches. They were getting her used to their touches and she found herself looking down and saw their cocks, already fully erected, continue to grow.

Cassidy's cock was flushed a deeper shade than Spencer's. Bigger than Spencer's too, with a giant mushroom shaped cockhead and bulging veins interlacing the entire length of his shaft. And Spencer's cock was tremendously thick and so long. The longest she'd ever seen. And both mens' scrotums were huge and swollen.

She reached out and took each of their sacs into her palms and held them. Squeezed and pinched them gently.

They both moaned in approval, their gazes flashing with desire. They kept touching her, their hands feathering over her hips, her thighs, her buttocks. She was creaming, her pleasure juices literally dripping along the insides of her thighs.

Their eyes became glazed as she played with their scrotums. Their breaths were harsh and loud. They smelled good too. Of the soap she'd left by the water pump and of fresh air.

They moved closer to her, their hips touching her, their hands roaming along her belly, her breasts.

"We were watching as Logan took you," Spencer said softly, his green eyes twinkling in the dim light.

Her tummy flipped with a wonderful feeling knowing they'd been there. They would know that something special had formed between Logan and herself. They would know she belonged to him. This time that last thought didn't seem at all impossible.

"You looked so hot dancing for him," Cassidy murmured. "We wanted to take you so bad, but we knew Logan wanted you even worse."

"Now you both have me," she whispered, feeling overwhelmed by their intimate touches, knowing that Logan was watching, waiting.

"Take me. Any way you want me."

She knew Logan would appreciate her offering herself to his friends. Pleasing him was the only thing she wanted to do right now. Funny, with Logan, she wanted him to pleasure her, but with the two guys, she wanted to please them.

And then Cassidy grabbed her around the wrist urging her to let go of his scrotum. Reluctantly she did and she whimpered as both men sheathed themselves in protection, Cassidy also lubing himself before he moved behind her, his hands coming to her waist like two hot brands. His generously lubed condom sheathed cock slid into her ass. She moaned and squirmed at the fierce pressure.

"Spread your legs wide," Spencer instructed. He dropped to his knees in front of her and leaned in, his warm breath caressing her pussy. She opened her legs to him and his head dipped in.

He parted her labia with his tongue and lapped at her juices, the bristly edges of his tongue feeling oh so fine. Then he sucked her clit into his hot mouth and massaged her with his tongue sending tremors raging through her, knocking her senses off balance, making her cry out and grab his shoulders for support.

"Man, wicked tight," Cassidy moaned from behind her as he withdrew and plunged his cock into her ass again.

Mercy, but he was huge, she thought and she hissed as he came out and sunk into her again. Between her legs, Spencer was lapping at her like crazy, rocking her world.

Then his mouth left her and he rubbed his hard body against hers as he stood. Cassidy withdrew and she heard him whisper something to Spencer. She wasn't sure what, because her ears were buzzing and her heart was thumping from the lust lashing her body. She cried out as Spencer's large cock slid into her wet pussy, sending pinpricks of pain and pleasure roaring through her. He impaled her balls deep and his luscious firm lips fused over hers, flaring nerves.

Both men began a mind shattering rhythm as they sandwiched her in the middle of them. One cock in, the other cock out. Their hips danced against hers with their every driving plunge, searing her closer to an orgasm.

Perspiration blossomed over her flesh and her body tightened, readying for the explosion of pleasure she was sure to come. But then they backed off, their thrusts slowing, leading her away from the edge of bliss.

They took her that way for a while, bringing her to the edge and then slowing their thrusts until her body tightened and neared climax and then they backed off again.

Finally, Spencer stopped kissing her and buried his mouth against the crevice of her neck and shoulder, his tongue lapping erotically against her sensitized flesh. She thought she heard Logan gasping nearby and opened her eyes to see him standing close; both his hands were quickly massaging his engorged cock. His gaze captured hers and held hers, sending signals for her to let herself go. To let herself enjoy these men who were taking her. It was strange that she would seek his permission to orgasm, but that's what she was doing.

The erotic sight of Logan, the fact that he was truly enjoying watching her having sex, had her creaming harder. Behind her, she could feel Cassidy's hands grip her waist firmer and Spencer's fingers curled tighter around her shoulders as they both bucked into her. Their bodies shivered and she cut herself loose too.

Closing her eyes, she exploded on a cry. Wave after wave of sheer pleasure cascaded over her, embraced her, loved her. The effects were so deep and so utterly wonderful, she literally felt her mind being sucked into a vortex of colors and her body torn apart by wrenching awesome convulsions. It was raw, blinding, and beautiful.

Perfect.

The three of them took turns with her through the night and it wasn't until the wee hours of the morning, they all flopped into her king-sized bed, exhausted. Logan spooned against her backside, while Spencer and Cassidy slept on her other side, snoring softly.

Logan gingerly stroked her hair, murmuring for her to get some sleep but despite feeling exhausted from all that delicious sex, sleep was the last thing she wanted.

"I don't want to go sleep," she confessed as she grabbed his hand and pulled it over her shoulder and onto her left breast.

He cupped her and held her. His hand was hot and felt so nice.

"You're tired. You should close your eyes and sleep," Logan urged.

She could hear the sleepiness in his voice too. Felt it tugging at her. Felt it pulling her under. She struggled against it. She truly did. But she felt as if she'd been drugged.

In a good way.

"I don't want you to go," she breathed.

She wasn't even sure she said it aloud. Maybe she was already asleep. Maybe she was already dreaming? She tightened her embrace on him. No, she didn't want him to go.

I don't want you to go.

Oh man, those words destroyed Logan and he knew they would haunt him for the rest of his life, Logan thought as his heart cracked painfully against his chest. He literally had to force himself not to tell her he would never leave her. No use in saying it. No use in lying.

He sighed heavily and winced as her fingers tightened around his wrist where she gripped him while he cupped her luscious breast.

Wow, but she had dammed good strength. Yeah, she was strong. She would survive out here. She'd survive without him. She had to.

Teyla knew they were gone the instant she sifted through the heavy layers of sleep that had kept her hostage in a land of black and peace. She swore she'd never slept so deeply. Swore she'd never felt as alive and happy as when she awoke. But the realization that the bed was empty and Logan was gone and that the rest of the money Logan owed her had been settled on the bed beside her so she wouldn't miss it, had ripped away her happiness and torn her heart apart.

Emotions, dark and deep slashed through her. Loss flooded her and she sobbed into her pillow most of the day and into that night.

But she was strong. She would survive this.

She had to.

Heart Creek...Two days later...

"Hands off Teyla Sutton or I cut off your balls. Understood?" Logan breathed against the son of a bitch banker and self-appointed lawman's ear. The man nodded eagerly but Logan pressed the barrel of his gun harder against the man's temple.

"If I ever hear that you've been sniffing around her again, word will get back to me. Rest assured if that happens your balls are mine. This money will pay in full what is owed to you by her. Understood? You stay away from her. Don't go to her place. Don't talk to her. Don't so much as look at her. Understood?"

Again, the man nodded eagerly, his big, pudgy body trembling against Logan. His long moustache tickling the side of Logan's chin.

Cassidy dropped the satchel of money onto the ground in front of the banker. The satchel contained their entire share of the loot from the heist minus what he'd left for Teyla, onto the dirt ground of the dark alley. The alley that Logan, Spencer, and Cassidy had dragged him into, after they'd identified the man, they'd been looking for.

"Sign this."

The man hesitated as Logan handed him a pen and thrust a paper in front of the guy's face.

"W...Where?"

"Use the wall." Logan nodded to Cassidy and Spencer who were still holding the man's arms tight, preventing him from escaping. They pushed him up against the wall and Logan placed the paper where the man had easy reach to it.

As he lifted his hand, it shook so badly, Logan feared he might not be able to sign the papers stating Teyla Sutton's mortgage was all paid off and no one had any further claim on her land. Logan had even gone as far as hiring the local lawyer, some young punk, who looked legitimate enough, to write up the proper legal form. Several townsfolk had vouched for his legitimacy.

Logan held his breath as the creep signed.

"And don't even think about saying you signed under duress. Or I'll cut off your cock along with your balls and hang my trophy off the side of my saddle. Understood? Now head back to your office and hire someone to ride out to her place and give her the deed, stating the land is hers, full and clear."

"Y...yes, sir. Yes sir," the man clambered.

"Remember, someone will be watching you. If you do something I don't like..." Logan let his warning words dangle in the frosty night air.

"Y...yes, sir...I...understand."

Logan nodded again and Spencer and Cassidy let him go. The banker raced off down the alley, falling twice over his shaking legs and never looking back. Logan didn't miss the fact a large wet spot appeared between the man legs. Obviously, the banker had wet his pants.

Good. The man should be scared.

"Do you think he'll follow through on your demands?" Cassidy asked as they watched him turn the corner and disappear.

"If he knows what's good for him." Logan said coolly. If the weasel so much as did anything to Teyla, Logan would make sure that creep was a dead man.

Epilogue

Eight months later...Valentine's Day

E It was the succulent scent of strawberries that dragged Teyla out of her sleep and when she opened her eyes, she saw the bunch of daisies, their delicate stems tied with a cute yellow ribbon, as well as a bowl of robust red strawberries staring her right in the face. At first, she thought she was having one heck of neat dream.

Daisies? Strawberries? Impossible. The strawberry plants in her greenhouse were just starting to grow. She'd finally gotten some plants only a couple of weeks ago. Dr. Elizabeth had brought them over, saying the grocery store in town was having a sale on them.

She knew Dr. Liz was lying. That store never had sales. She knew that fact when she went to town with the black horse Logan had left her. The same black horse he'd come to her home with on that chilly evening. But she'd accepted the gift from Liz and planted the strawberry plants thinking about Logan the whole time. Thinking about how she'd told him she wanted strawberry plants and how she would love to eat some strawberry shortcake.

What a silly frivolous thing for her to say to him. He must have thought her impractical in mentioning something like that. Especially with this cold winter. She swore it had been the coldest one yet.

Dr. Liz had been doing that a lot. Checking up on her. Bless her heart. Teyla had poured her heart out to Dr. Liz, telling her about Logan and what had happened with Cassidy and Spencer and how devastated she'd been when they'd left. The doctor had been a savior and Teyla wasn't sure what she'd have done if she hadn't had the woman to confide in.

The blow of Logan leaving hadn't been eased when a couple of days after they'd left, she'd found the deed to her property nailed to her front door, stating her property had been paid in full. She knew in her heart Logan, Cassidy and Spencer had had something to do with it.

Since then, she hadn't seen the banker come here. The couple of times she'd gone to town, he'd made a big circle around her avoiding her like the plague. Knowing her property belonged to her was liberating. Knowing she was now in debt to Logan and possibly Spencer and Cassidy should have made her upset. Curiously, it didn't. She was grateful and considered them her heroes.

Speaking of heroes, what was up with these daisies and the strawberries? Surely, she was dreaming.

Wasn't she?

She closed her eyes and opened them again.

Still there.

Had she lost her mind?

Definitely.

She didn't know how long she stared at the flowers and the strawberries. It couldn't have been very long, because soon she smelled something else.

Smelled *him*.

No. God couldn't be so cruel as to have her dreaming about Logan. Not again. She went through this almost every night since he'd been gone. Dreaming he was here.

Movement from the corner of her eyes caught her attention and alarm snapped through her. Someone was here!

Instantly she reached beneath her pillow, grabbing the loaded gun she kept there for such emergencies. In a split second she'd palmed it, released the safety catch and she was halfway up into a seated position, pointing the gun at the movement when she saw the familiar figure standing at the window.

He'd opened the curtains and was peering out.

"Logan?" she breathed and blinked wildly, trying to orient herself.

This wasn't possible. She'd given up on him ever coming back. She'd convinced herself it had been a one-way attraction. All hers.

She'd figured she'd only romanticized about him because she'd been lonely. Thought he'd paid off her farm because that's what he did now for a living. Stole from the rich to give to others.

She didn't agree with how she figured the property had been paid for, with stolen money, but what could she do about it? She didn't want to return to having that bastard showing up at her place whenever he wanted and demanding sex from her again.

Heck, she hadn't even been able to accept another client into her bed because of Logan.

When Logan turned from the window and he spied the gun in her hand, his brows rose in surprise.

"I guess I shouldn't have stayed away so long. It looks like your taste in bed companions has changed and not for the better."

He grinned that wonderful tummy flipping grin that just about made her leap out of bed and jump into his arms. She stopped herself short but she couldn't stop herself from smiling and shaking her head.

The man still had a sense of humor. Still sexy looking as ever in his tight jeans and this time he wore a light green tee shirt that prominently illuminated the abundance of muscles in his arms and chest. Best of all he was wearing that gorgeous five o'clock shadow that she loved on his face. He looked so yummy she wanted to have him for breakfast. And lunch. And dinner. And always.

She held herself back. Tried not to let the happiness bubble through her like an untapped spring. He was probably only back for sex. And then he'd be gone again. She shouldn't accept him this time. She should tell him she would pay him back in installments and send him packing. Even as she thought about doing just that, concern whipped through her as he stepped away from the window and closer to her.

"You look tired," she whispered, stunned at the dark circles hanging beneath his eyes. He looked thinner too.

"I missed you like you wouldn't believe. I tried to stay away, but we finally caved and we broke from the Gang."

We finally caved? What was he talking about? Her mind must still be sleep muddled because she thought he'd said he missed her.

"When did you come in?"

"Now," he whispered and he began to undress.

What? What was he saying? Her heart crashed against her chest as a moment later he stood before her totally naked and fully erect. He lifted the daisies and the plate of strawberries off the pillow and settled them onto the nearby dresser.

"I couldn't find strawberry shortcake, so I brought the next best thing, strawberries. And since you deserve flowers every morning, I will bring them to you, even if I have to go a hundred miles every day. But all that can wait because I'm coming in, now," he said as he climbed into bed beside her and took her into his strong arms, crushing her to his strong chest.

He held her there for so long she thought maybe he would stay like this forever.

Finally, she was able to formulate a semblance of the question she knew she had to ask before she let anything else happen between them. If he came up with the wrong answer, she knew she would have to ask him to leave and never come back.

"How long are you staying?"

"Forever. If you want me to."

"Spencer and Cassidy?" She knew he loved sharing. Wanted to please him. Wanted more of those scorching ménages she'd experienced with them too.

"They'll be by tomorrow and they won't be leaving either."
Yeah! Right answer.

The End

The Desperadoes Series~MFMM

~
Erotic Romance, Futuristic Sci-Fi, MÉNAGE À QUATRE, M/F/M/
M
A fiery eruption of solar flares disintegrates much of the world's
population, fries electrical grids, and throws Earth back into the dark
ages. Now, it's a cold, brutal land where only the strong survive.

The Pleasure Girl
The Desperadoes Book One

AFTER THE CATASTROPHE, Teyla Sutton becomes a pleasure girl, entertaining men on her secluded Canadian farm. When she accommodates dangerous desperado, Logan Leigh and his two friends, Spencer and Cassidy, pleasure becomes addictive beneath their tender touches and their hard, muscular bodies. What she never expects is to fall in love...

Logan shouldn't allow the pleasure girl into his heart, but he knows it's too late because she's already there. He and his friends have put their lives into danger by hiding out at her farm. They're on the run. They need to leave, yet Logan wants her so much. Dare he risk his heart and their lives to be with her?

Soon Logan, Cassidy and Spencer are whisking Teyla away on an exquisite journey into her hottest desires and forbidden fantasies. But when she learns the trio are members of a notorious outlaw gang, can she allow them to stay in her life, or will she send them away forever?

In Her Bed
The Desperadoes Series Book 2

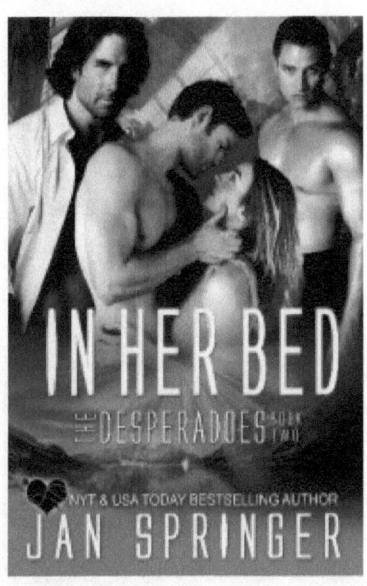

A fiery eruption of solar flares disintegrates much of the world's population, fries electrical grids, and throws Earth back into the dark ages. Now, it's a cold, brutal land where only the strong survive.

Before the Catastrophe, Dr. Elizabeth Brandywine would never have dreamed of surrendering to her wicked needs of being bound, dominated, and shared, but now there's no one left alive to judge her, except herself.

Ethan Durango knows sweet, uptight, sexy Dr. Liz is ready to submit to her secret most intimate needs. He's always wanted to share her and Ethan, Landon, and Tyrell will enjoy pushing Liz past her boundaries until she submits to her naughtiest desires.

EROTIC ROMANCE, FUTURISTIC Sci-Fi, MÉNAGE À QUATRE, M/F/M/M, BDSM, sex toys.

Awakening Eve
The Desperadoes Series Book Three

Passionate ménages with the fierce men of the Durango gang have always made Eve Wright's body hum with sizzling arousal. Secretly, she loved all three men, that is, until she suffered a head injury and forgot them.

Now her memory is returning with a carnal vengeance and she knows of only one way to relieve her most intimate frustrations...by returning to the men she once loved.

When Eve shows up at their hideout, Kayne, Riley, and Maddox are pleased she wants them to help her remember what they once shared. Their hot looks, tender touches, and scorching pleasure will leave Eve tangled in an erotic storm that threatens to break her heart and give up a gut-wrenching secret.

Erotic Romance, Futuristic Sci-Fi, MÉNAGE À QUATRE, M/F/M/M, bondage, sex toys

Cowboys Online Series~ MFMM

Contemporary Western Romance
~ Jan Springer ~ Erotic Romance ~

Cowboys for Christmas

Cowboys Online 1 ~ Moose Ranch
Jennifer Jane (JJ) Watson has spent the past ten Christmases in a
maximum-security prison.
The last thing she expects is to get early parole, along with a job on a
remote Canadian cattle ranch serving Christmas holiday dinners to
three of the sexiest cowboys she's ever met!
Rafe, Brady and Dan thought they were getting a couple of male
ex-cons to help out around their secluded ranch, but instead they get
an attractive and very appealing female.
In the snowbound wilds of Northern Ontario, female companionship
is rare.
It's a good thing the three men like to share...
They're dominating, sexy-as-sin and they fill JJ with the hottest
ménage fantasies she's ever had. Suddenly she's craving cowboys for
Christmas and wishing for something she knows she can never have...a
happily ever after.

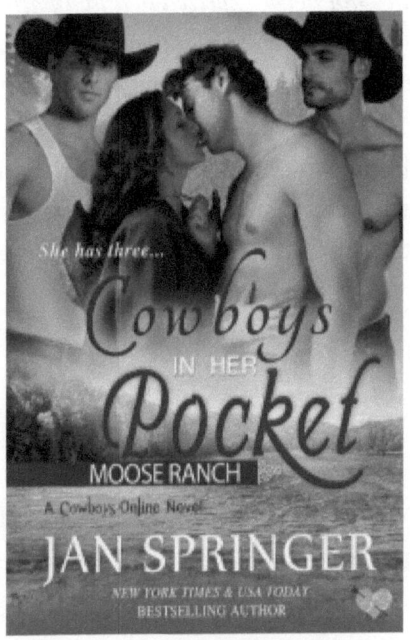

Cowboys In Her Pocket
Cowboys Online 2 ~ Moose Ranch
Jan Springer

*After spending ten years in a maximum-security prison Jennifer Jane (JJ)
Watson got early parole and a job on a remote Canadian cattle ranch
playing housekeeper to three of the sexiest cowboys she's ever met...*

Spring has finally arrived at Moose Ranch, and a single woman fresh
out of prison shouldn't be experiencing scorching ménages with her
three sexy-as-sin cowboys. But JJ's love for her men continues to grow
as she gives into the fevered heat and scorching passions she feels for
each of them.

Life is perfect.

Until her new life is tested when mysterious happenings occur on the
ranch and then one of her cowboys is viciously attacked and injured.

Will JJ's newfound freedom and happiness be ripped away?

Rafe, Brady and Dan never expected to find an attractive and very appealing female to help them out at their secluded ranch. But in the wilds of Northern Ontario, female companionship is rare. It's a good thing the three men like to share...

Brady, Dan and Rafe have never been happier. Their cattle ranch is flourishing and their continued desire to share the sexy woman who cares for them makes their life complete. Until danger threatens to rip everything apart...

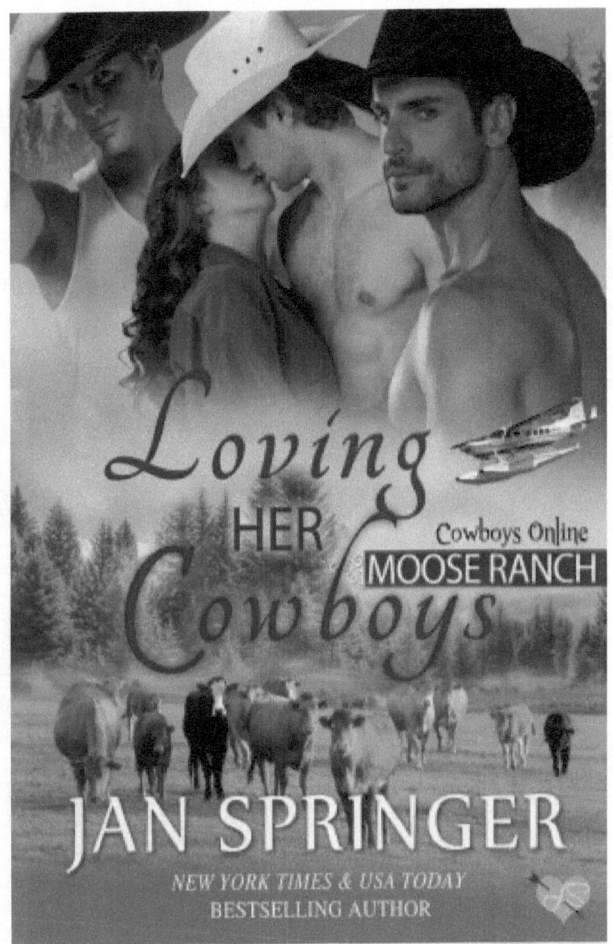

Loving Her Cowboys
Cowboys Online 3 ~ Moose Ranch
Jan Springer

*AFTER SPENDING TEN years in a maximum-security prison Jennifer
Jane (JJ) Watson got early parole and a job on a remote Canadian cattle
ranch playing housekeeper to three of the sexiest cowboys she's ever met...*

Her love for her cowboys continues to grow as she gives into
fevered heat. But JJ's simmering restlessness explodes and she's seriously
making up for lost time by pursuing her dreams. There's only one little
problem. She hasn't revealed to her bosses what she's been up to while

they're away tending to the cattle. She knows when they discover her secret, there will be hell to pay.

Ranchers Rafe, Dan and Brady have found the woman who completes them. She makes their secluded ranch a home-sweet-home. She's vulnerable, sweet and willing to share her bed with all three of them. But when JJ's secret is unwittingly revealed, they're stunned and angry. They figure it's time to dole out some fiery punishment in some mighty naughty ways...

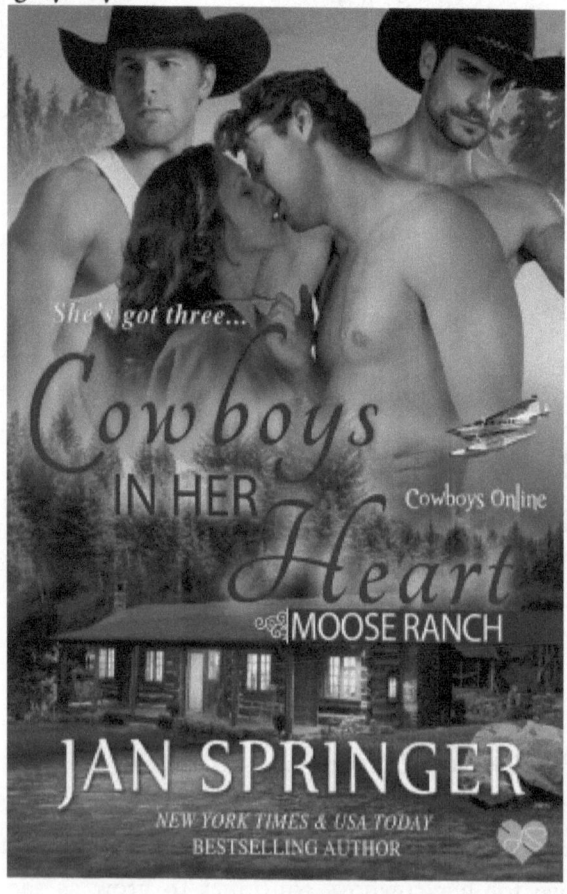

Cowboys In Her Heart

Cowboys Online 4 ~ Moose Ranch
Jan Springer

AFTER SPENDING TEN years in a maximum-security prison, JJ gets unexpected parole and a job on a Canadian ranch serving up scrumptious dinners and lots of hot love to three of the sexiest cowboys she's ever met.

Jennifer Jane "JJ" Watson has never been happier. She's going to have a baby!

Thankfully their wilderness ranch is a nice distraction for her three sexy cowboys while she's away flying her plane. But when she's home, her dominant hunks are tending to her naughty pregnant cravings and that includes plenty of sizzling ménages.

Rafe, Brady and Dan don't much like the idea of their woman flying the Canadian skies and being at the mercy of the unpredictable Northern Ontario weather. They would prefer having her warming their beds twenty-four seven. But she has a way of getting what she wants and right now she needs her new-found freedom.

Worst fears are realized when JJ, her friend and JJ's plane suddenly go missing and she doesn't come back home to them.

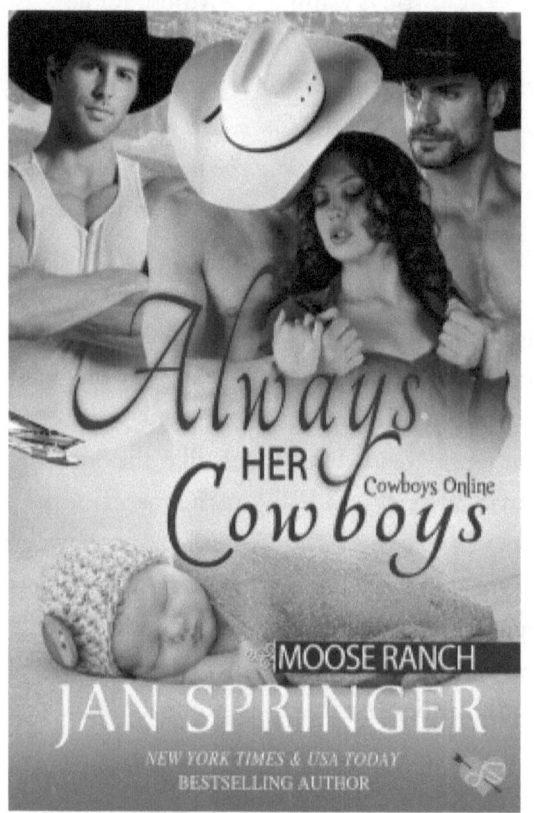

Always Her Cowboys
Cowboys Online 5 ~ Moose Ranch
A Canadian Contemporary Ménage Romance m/f/m/m

JENNIFER JANE (JJ) Watson has spent ten Christmases in a maximum-security prison. The last thing she expects is to get early parole, along with a job on a remote Canadian cattle ranch serving Christmas holiday dinners to three of the sexiest cowboys she's ever met!

Rafe, Brady and Dan thought they were getting male ex-cons to help out around their secluded ranch, but instead they get an attractive and very appealing female. In the snowbound wilds of Northern Ontario, female companionship is rare. It's a good thing the three men like to share...

Christmas is coming once again to Moose Ranch and with the due date of JJ's baby approaching fast, JJ is distracting herself from anxiety attacks by keeping herself ultra-busy preparing for the arrival of her baby and planning Moose Ranch's first annual Christmas party!

In having a wee baby on the way, there's a lot of stress for Brady, Rafe and Dan. Especially due to JJ's decision on having a wilderness mid-wife deliver the baby at the ranch house - *with* all *of them present for the birth*! But their concerns don't stop the men from showing JJ how much they love her...out of bed and in!

With wicked snowstorms, a grounded bush plane, a cheerful holiday party and a sweet little baby, the owners of Moose Ranch know this will be one sparkling Christmas season they won't soon forget...

Her Forever Cowboys ~ Snowy Creek Ranch #1
Cowboys Online #6

After spending years in prison, Milena Allen is unexpectedly paroled and given a job at a secluded Canadian horse ranch where she's instantly attracted to her three sexy cowboy bosses!

When Cowboys Online sends Mitch, Daegen and Paul a cute female ex-con to help out around their fledgling wilderness ranch, they realize life has been awfully lonesome without female companionship.

Despite being without women for so long, they vow Milena is off limits, and they will treat her like one of the guys.

When violence threatens her cowboys, Milena's nursing skills are put to the test, and she realizes she's falling head over cowboy boots for her sexy bosses. Soon she discovers all three men are interested in her too! But they keep treating her like one of the guys!

She's always dreamed for someone to love her and for a place she can call home. Will Mitch, Daegen and Paul make her dreams come true? Or will a horrific mistake unravel everything?

Please note you do not need to read the other books in the series. This book can stand alone.

Cowboys Online Series ~ Book One – Cowboys for Christmas (Moose Ranch), Book Two – Cowboys in Her Pocket (Moose Ranch), Book Three – Loving Her Cowboys (Moose Ranch), Book Four – Cowboys In Her Heart (Moose Ranch), Book Five – Always Her Cowboys (Moose Ranch), Book Six – Her Forever Cowboys (Snowy Creek Ranch).

Jan Springer Mini Catalog

Step into The Key Club's Ménage Nights where naughty fantasies come true and two men are hotter than one. Includes FIVE bestselling The Key Club stories; Ménage, Marley's Ménage, A Merry Ménage Christmas, Sophie's Ménage and Jewel's Ménage.

The Key Club Series
Ménage - Book One

Sandwiched between constant deadlines, erotic romance author Claire Miller, enjoys an occasional unwind at The Key Club. And this time she's going to indulge in a yummy ménage.
Marley's Ménage - Book Two

Single soon-to-be mom Marley Madison has had some wicked cravings in her day but being pregnant has made her cravings downright naughty. She wants a sizzling ménage, and she needs it bad.

A Merry Ménage Christmas - Book Three

Dr. Kelsie Madison can't remember the last time she's had no-strings sex, and that's her clue she's been working way too hard. It's time to unwind at the Key Club by indulging in a yummy Christmas present for herself...a red-hot ménage.

Sophie's Ménage - Book Four

It's Spank-Me Ménage Night at the Key Club and Sophie is finally taking the plunge back into the spank scene...but she didn't expect her two ex-boyfriends to be there too.

Jewel's Ménage - Book Five

SHE THOUGHT SHE WOULD never trust a man again...

Until one rainy night, two hunky truckers come to Jewel's rescue, igniting delicious desires for a red-hot Ménage à trois

Jaxie's Ménage - Book Six

A close encounter with death pushes Jaxie into making one of her most intimate fantasies come true...

A Homecoming Ménage Christmas - Book Seven

Rachel has a very naughty secret, and she's way too embarrassed to let anyone know about it. When The Key Club throws a Santa Fetish Ménage Night, it's almost too good to be true. She has to figure out how to participate without anyone finding out!

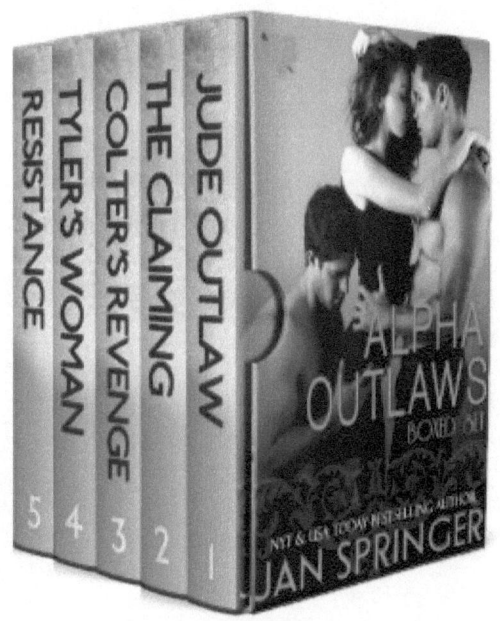

Alpha Outlaws Boxed Set
The Outlaw Lovers (Books 1 - 5)

A FAST-ACTING VIRUS has killed a majority of the world's female population. With so few women on Earth, a new law is created. The Claiming Law allow groups of men to stake a claim on a female—as their sensual property.

The Outlaw brothers have full intentions of declaring ownership of the women they love...and they'll do it any way they can.

This boxed set contains the first FIVE books in The Outlaw Lovers series.

Jude Outlaw, The Claiming, Colter's Revenge, Tyler's Woman, Resistance,

Some scenes include scorching ménages, romances, light bondage, bdsm, m/f/m/m, m/f, m/f/m, m/m, anal, oral, double penetration, figging, and more...

Please note: Tyler's Woman Book 4 in this series is not for sensitive readers.

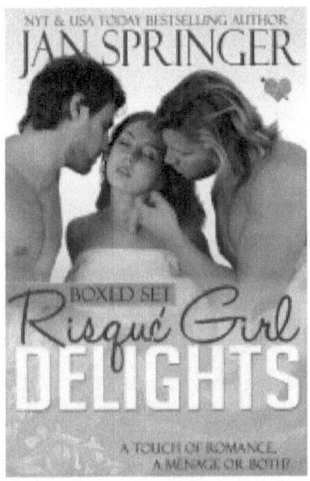

Risqué Girl Delights Box Set
Jan Springer

A sizzling set of 4 contemporary erotic romances...Four women dare
to step out of the norm in the Risqué Girl Delights Boxed Set.
Includes sexy romances, naughty ménages, toys and hot alpha males.
Books: Edible Delights, Toygasm, Shy Girl, plus Roman & Julietta.

Edible Delights
YEARS AGO ALLIE MASTERS lost herself in the scorching passion
of a ménage a trois relationship with her two bosses. In order to regain
her independence, she walked away.

Max and Nick were very fulfilled with their gorgeous assistant. The lovemaking was breathtaking and both men willingly shared the woman they wanted to spend the rest of their lives with. Then she left.

Now Max and Nick have decided it's time to seduce Allie back into their lives.

Toygasm

IT'S A CASE OF MISTAKEN identity when the two owners of Sexy Toys, show up for an erotic several day photo shoot of their toys with famous nude model Cammie Creek.

Cammie believes the two hunks are the male models she's supposed to work with. Usually she doesn't mix business with pleasure, but when they're seducing her right there in front of the camera, she can't resist turning them into her own personal naughty toys.

Josh and Jode are enjoying the perks of being male models; hot lust, sizzling toys and the best pleasure they've ever had. But how will Cammie react when she discovers they're actually her bosses and not just male models?

Shy Girl

FINALLY FREE OF AN abusive relationship, "Shy Girl" Emma McCall sheds her inhibitions and explores her sensual side at Club Rendezvous, a club specializing in the Alternate Lifestyle.

At the club she's surprised to find Logan Masters, a sexy hunk she's secretly fantasized about since college. With Logan's help, Emma will experience her ultimate fantasy - a scorching ménage a trois.

Roman and Julietta

HER PERFECT LOVER...

Modern day pirate Julietta Black's life has always been immersed in the violent and traditional ways of piracy. When her family's arch enemy puts a hit out on her family, Julietta knows there's only one way to lift the hit; she must kidnap the enemy's sexy grandson and force a union between the two warring families. Night after night, wrapped in Roman's strong arms, she can't deny the searing attraction blazing between them. Nor can she deny he now holds her heart as well as her life in his hands.

His dream angel...

When Roman Prince's mysterious captor offers him a luscious woman to bed, fierce desire ignites, melting his usually tight self-control. Lust quickly turns to love as he enjoys their naughty trysts more than he should. How will he react when he discovers he's been kidnapped, not for a ransom, but captured for his sperm?

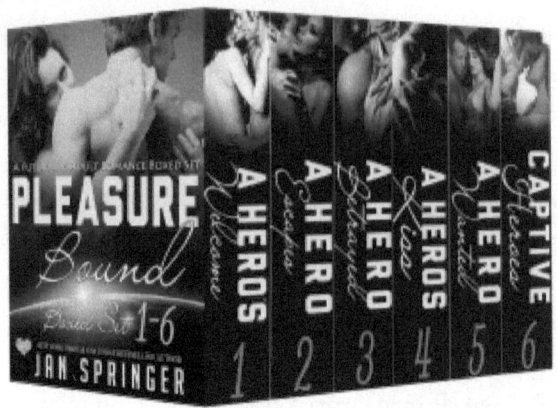

Futuristic Erotic Romance (m/f)
Pleasure Bound ~ The Complete Set ~ Books 1-6
Jan Springer

A HERO'S WELCOME – Book One – Dr. Annie welcomes injured astronaut Joe Hero into her bed every chance she gets.

A Hero Escapes – Book Two – Queen Jacey's forbidden fantasies become reality and she can't get enough of well-hung Ben Hero's sizzling lovemaking.

A Hero Betrayed – Book Three – Fugitive-on-the-run Virgin must save Buck Hero who has been infected by a deadly virus. The cure? A twenty-four-hour making love marathon! But then she must betray him...

A Hero's Kiss – Book Four – US Astronaut Piper Hero is rescued by a dangerous stranger and can't seem to keep her hands off his luscious whip-scarred body.

A Hero Wanted – Book Five – A Hero is wanted for plus-sized Jenna who is finally able to explore her intimate side...where ménages are welcome.

Captive Heroes – Book Six – While searching for her brothers, Kayla Hero is bound and imprisoned by the Breeders— along with a male captive whose tantalizing scars pique her interest.

Injured and lost in a dense jungle, Kinley Hero is intimidated by the scarred man who hunts her, especially due to the power of erotic submission he holds over her.

Naughty Girl Desires Boxed Set
Contemporary Erotic Romance (m/f)
Includes: Jade's Fantasy, The Biker & The Bride,
Sinderella Sexy and Nice Girl Naughty.

Jade's Fantasy
In the land of the rich and famous, Kidnap Fantasies is the answer to discreet naughty downtime.
When ex-downhill skier Jade Hart's two sisters give her a Kidnap Fantasies questionnaire, Jade is aroused at the prospect of having no-strings fun in the sun with a stranger whose only job would be to fulfill her every intimate fantasy. Although she knows she's too shy to send it in, she secretly pours her deepest wishes into the questionnaire. Soon the questionnaire mysteriously vanishes and Jade's fantasy man appears on her luxury yacht in the form of a sexy handy man who gives her an intimate toy-filled Christmas holiday she'll never forget.

The Biker & The Bride
Wrapped in red-hot lust for revenge, Avery plots to murder the man responsible for the death of her son.
Her plans are dashed when her ex-husband crashes her wedding and whisks her away on his motorcycle to the rustic Canadian wilderness cabin they'd once honeymooned.
Police detective, Mason is fighting for Avery's love with everything he has.
Armed with whipped cream, handcuffs and his undying devotion, Mason vows he will make Avery love again.
But it's only a matter of time before the man she'd planned to kill hunts them down...

Sinderella Sexy

By night, Dr. Ella Cinder, escapes reality by secretly performing in her own naughty version of Cinderella, aptly re-titled Sinderella. When sexy colleague Dr. Roarke Stephenson appears in the Sinderella audience on the same night her Prince Charming stands her up, Ella Cinder seizes the opportunity to make the man she's secretly fantasized about into her very own Prince Charming for one night of carnal fun in front of an audience.

But at the stroke of midnight, Ella knows she must face the harsh reality that Roarke can never learn her true identity.

Dr. Roarke Stephenson is immediately captured by the mysterious actress who hides her face behind a mask and is known only as Sinderella. For some insane reason, she reminds him of his klutzy co-worker, Ella. But that's not possible. Plain Ella would never have the nerve to do the wickedly delicious things Sinderella does to him, or would she?

Nice Girl Naughty

Blind since nineteen, Summer has blossomed into a famous wood carver.

When she's almost killed by a serial killer, she's whisked away to a secluded wilderness cabin by the man she once secretly loved.

Summer can't get enough of touching professional bodyguard Nick Cassidy's thick, powerful muscles and all those other hard, yummy male body parts that she has always longed to explore.

For years Nick has stayed away from his best friend's kid sister, nice girl Summer. Now he's back, and sweeping his gorgeous redhead into the naughty cravings he's always had for her. With passion blinding him, Nick doesn't realize their hideout isn't safe—until it's too late.

YOU CAN GET A PEEK at more of Jan Springer's Erotic Romances at:

    http://www.janspringer.com[1]

Jasmine Black ~Erotica

Here are some Jasmine Black ebooks...

Taken by Three Billionaires

Billionaire friends, Liam, Theo and Elijah have just won Princess Isabella in a billionaire card game. Isabella knows exactly what the three men will want from her...she just hadn't expected to have all three of them at once!

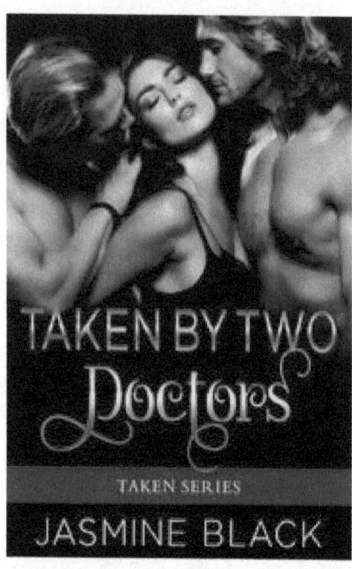

Taken by Two Doctors
A BDSM Medical Fetish Erotica Quickie MFM

Waitress Jean Spelling visits her controversial doctor once a month for
some much-needed...stress relief. She looks forward to putting her feet
up in the stirrups and enjoys Dr. Ball's naughty unconventional
treatments. This time when she arrives, she's surprised to discover that
she'll be physically examined by two doctors and they'll prescribe her
some much-needed release right there on the examination table!

eBooks in the Ménage series
Taken by Three Bikers
Taken by Three Billionaires
Taken by Three Doctors
Taken by Three Cowboys

eBooks in the Taken series
Taken by Two Firefighters
Taken by Two Bikers
Taken by Two Billionaires
Taken by Two Bosses
Taken by Two Cowboys
Taken by Two Personal Trainers
Taken by Two Carpenters

Jasmine Black Website ~ http://www.jasmine-black.com
Twitter ~ @blackerotica1

Jasmine Black has an Erotic Romance Side...Jan Springer

Merry Menage Kisses BoxSet
...getting down and naughty

Wrap yourself in these four sexy holiday themed adult romance ménages to sizzle your Christmas reading.

A Homecoming Menage Christmas ~ Rachel has a secret Santa fetish and she'll be getting two Santas for Christmas.
A Merry Menage Christmas ~ All work and no play encourages Dr. Kelsie Madison to get herself a sizzling ménage this holiday season.

Cowboys for Christmas ~ After spending the last ten Christmases in prison, Jennifer Jane is getting three hot Canadian cowboys for Christmas.

Christmas Lovers ~ A soldier and his nurse are falling in love and a naughty Christmas gift will ignite their passions at a mountain chalet.

Happy Holidays!

Here are ways we can connect:

Jasmine Black Website at http://janspringerauthor.wordpress.com/jasmine-black/

Jan Springer Website at http://www.janspringer.com[1]

Instagram – http://www.instagram.com/janspringerauthor

Facebook - https://www.facebook.com/janspringereroticromance

Twitter Jan Springer- https://twitter.com/janspringer @janspringer

Twitter Jasmine Black - https://twitter.com/blackerotica1 @blackerotica1

Pinterest - http://www.pinterest.com/janspringer2/

Jan's Blog - http://janspringerauthor.wordpress.com/blog-2/

Happy Reading,

Jasmine Black / Jan Springer

---

1.   http://www.janspringer.com/